Caught in the Act

Also by Sara Jane Stone

Full Exposure
Command Performance

Caught in the Act

BOOK TWO: INDEPENDENCE FALLS

SARA JANE STONE

AVONIMPULSE
An Imprint of HarperCollinsPublishers

Excerpt from *The Cowboy and the Angel* copyright © 2014 by Tina Klinesmith.

Excerpt from *Finding Miss McFarland* copyright © 2014 by Vivienne Lorret.

Excerpt from *Take the Key and Lock Her Up* copyright © 2014 by Lena Diaz.

Excerpt from *Dylan's Redemption* copyright © 2014 by Jennifer Ryan.

Excerpt from *Sinful Rewards 1* copyright © 2014 by Cynthia Sax.

Excerpt from *Whatever It Takes* copyright © 2014 by Dixie Brown.

Excerpt from *Hard to Hold On To* copyright © 2014 by Laura Kaye.

Excerpt from *Kiss Me, Captain* copyright © 2014 by Gwen T. Weerheim-Jones.

EPub Edition SEPTEMBER 2014 ISBN: 9780062337597
Print Edition ISBN: 9780062337634

10 9 8 7 6 5 4 3 2 1

*To my family, who has always supported
my desire to write—I love you.*

Acknowledgments

I HAVE A long list of people in Oregon to thank. Diana and Larry Blair—I could not have written this book without you. Larry, your insights into the timber industry, and your introductions, were priceless. Diana, you're hands down the best mother-in-law. Thank you for watching the kids while I wrote. I am also in debt to Terry Lamers of Lamers Forests Ltd. Thank you for the tour of your forest!

Monica and Dave Jelden, every time I talk to you, I'm inspired to write. Thank you for introducing the idea of biomass fuel. (I bet you never thought that conversation over wine one night would become part of my story!) Any mistakes are my own.

In many ways, my books are a team effort. Thank you to Jill Marsal at the Marsal Lyon Literary Agency for always pushing me to write better stories. Amanda Bergeron, you are amazing! Your editorial comments truly took this book to another level. The talented team at Avon—everyone who had a hand in launching this series—deserves a huge thank-you, and possibly a bottle of bubbly.

To my readers, I love your enthusiasm for my stories and I hope to see you on Facebook again soon!

Chapter 1

THUMP, THUMP, THUMP. Katie Summers knew she had found trouble. Steering her station wagon to the shoulder, she glanced in the rearview mirror—and saw her passengers gnawing on the backseat. She wasn't sure if she should be relieved they weren't butting their horns against the car doors or alarmed that the inside of her station wagon would soon match the falling-apart exterior.

"Stop," she said, her voice firm.

Two of the orphaned goats that she'd picked up while scouting locations for her friend Georgia's bachelorette party ignored her. The third, the youngest of the bunch and the only girl, looked at her, and then back at her brothers, as if trying to decide who should have the final say. The big brothers won and the baby goat reached for the seat belt.

Outside the car, the thumping continued. Katie

sighed. She'd blown a tire. Slowing the wagon to a stop, she cut the engine and climbed out to take a look. Standing with her hands on her hips, she surveyed the damage.

Shredded tire? Check.

Bent rim? Check.

She moved to the rear of the car and opened the trunk, silently cursing her fitted green sundress and strappy sandals. It was the perfect outfit for an early fall trip to visit vineyards and other potential venues in and around Independence Falls, but she'd rather have her cowboy boots and jeans for fixing her car.

"Don't even think about trying to escape," she said, staring down her four-legged passengers. Pulling the spare tire out of the truck, she quickly closed the rear door and set the spare beside her wagon. She'd forgotten the jack, dammit.

Returning to the trunk, she opened it and began searching through the extra horse gear and other random farm supplies she kept in the station wagon. The animals ignored her, preferring to destroy her car than try to escape.

"Where is it?" Her brothers always made sure she had a jack in her car. When it came to interfering with her life, overprotective was the tip of the iceberg when it came to her older siblings. And road safety? They drove and maintained a fleet of trucks for a living. They would never let her leave the house without a spare, a jack, and flares. Just in case.

She heard a loud rip and glanced up to see one of the boy goats holding a large chunk of her backseat.

"Stop that," she said.

But the roar of a motorcycle drowned out her words and the sound of the goats tearing apart the wagon's interior. She waited for it to pass her. But instead it slowed, then cut out altogether.

Everyone in Independence Falls knew her station wagon. Nine out of ten residents would stop to offer a hand. Most would probably worry what her brothers would do if they found out someone had driven past her.

But just in case this wasn't a friendly face from her Oregon small town, Katie reached for the nearest heavy object—the jack, *finally*—and prepared to swing it at the person on the bike. Her brothers had taught her more than how to change a tire. If this guy made a wrong move, she'd make sure he regretted it.

One hand on the jack and the other pressed against the floor of the trunk, Katie glanced over her shoulder.

"No, no, no," she murmured. "Not you."

Wearing a black leather jacket and blue jeans that casually hugged his muscular legs, Liam Trulane sat upright on his bike, his work boots resting on the ground. He pulled off his helmet, revealing his wavy brown hair. And just like that, her mind stumbled into the past.

"Come here, honey." His deep brown eyes promised erotic adventure. He held out a hand, the muscles in his toned arms begging to be touched. "Now."

Katie obeyed, swinging one leg over his thighs and settling onto his lap. She felt the hard ridge of his erection against her despite the layers of clothing...

Katie ground her teeth together, pushing the mental

picture away. Maybe later, when she was alone, she would revisit the Liam Trulane highlight reel. But right now she'd be damned if this man saw even a hint of desire in her eyes.

She tolerated Liam Trulane. Mainly because his little sister, Georgia, had become Katie's closest friend. But that's where Katie drew the line. And she refused to let memories cloud her judgment. After what he'd done, the way he'd ended things between them, she deserved to hold tight to her anger.

Setting the helmet on the back of his bike, Liam reached for the zipper on his leather jacket, slowly drawing it down. But Katie didn't need a glimpse beneath to confirm that he possessed a powerful upper body—one that made women across the Willamette Valley connect the word "logger" with "longing to touch."

The tension in her jaw rippled through her body. At one point, she'd been one of those foolish girls. But not anymore. Now she connected this particular logger with one word. Betrayal.

Liam smiled as if he hadn't cut apart her heart, shredded her trust, and then walked away. Maybe the years had dulled his memory. They had only sharpened hers.

"I thought this was your wagon." He dismounted the bike in one fluid motion, resting it on the kickstand. "Breakdown?"

She stood, still holding the jack. Her free hand smoothed her skirt. It figured that after all this time he'd catch her bent over with her dress riding up the backs of her legs. Judging from the way his gaze followed her hands, he was picturing all the ways he could use her short skirt to his advantage.

But Liam Trulane didn't need to imagine.

Hands and knees pressing into the grass, her short skirt decorating her waist, her body waiting for his touch, needing it, craving it, silently hoping he would take charge as he'd done every other time. Following his commands, she could pretend this wasn't new to her. . .

"Flat tire." She punctuated her words with the slam of the trunk and moved to the side of the car. Kneeling down, she set up the jack.

"You're not going to need that."

Out of the corner of her eye, she spotted Liam's tan boots standing beside her. "Planning to lift my wagon with your superpowers?"

"Honey, even I'm not that talented."

No, you're not. She wished she could say those words out loud—and mean them.

"Your spare is flat," he added.

Abandoning the jack, Katie stood, dusting the roadside dirt off her knees, and looked at the tire she'd hauled from her trunk. Damn him, he was right. That tire wouldn't make it the three miles to her family home.

"I have an extra helmet if you want a ride."

She shook her head. There was no way she was getting on his motorcycle. The thought of his thighs nestled between hers, her chest against his back, and her arms wrapped around him, all while the motorcycle vibrated beneath them—it was hot, tempting, and downright impossible.

"No. If I show up on the back of your bike, my brothers will start throwing punches." She turned to face Liam. He'd crossed his arms in front of his chest. Even with the leather jacket on, she could see the bulge of his biceps. He could probably land a few hits himself. But he wouldn't. If it resembled the last fight she'd witnessed between her siblings and Liam, he'd take the hits. "And while that's tempting—"

"You want your brothers to pick a fight?"

She shrugged. "Better than inviting you in for a beer and a game of pool."

She'd dumped her last three boyfriends when they started spending more time hanging out with her brothers than with her. But this was Liam. The chances of her brothers shooting the shit with him were slim. As far as she knew, they hadn't forgiven him. There wasn't much she and her brothers agreed on these days. But when it came to their long-standing grudge against Liam Trulane? She knew her brothers were on her side.

"When they hear it was either a ride with me or standing on the side of the road in a cell phone dead zone, unable to call for help, I think they'll offer me the beer."

"Your what?" Hands dropped to his side as he peered into her wagon. "What the hell are you doing dressed up and driving around with livestock in your car?"

"I was looking at potential spots for Georgia's bachelorette."

Liam looked at her, eyebrows raised. "You're throwing my little sister a party that involves goats?"

"They were at one of the venues. The owner was planning to take them to the slaughterhouse. Even the baby. So I bought them. And we are *not* having Georgia's party there."

He looked at her as if she'd exchanged her common sense for the animals currently eating her car. And she suspected her brothers' reaction would match Liam's what-am-I-going-to-do-with-you expression.

"Guess I'm walking you home."

"No. I'll be fine on my own."

"I'm not letting you go alone, Katie."

He turned and headed for his motorcycle. Her eyes narrowed and she debated picking up the flat spare and tossing it at him. He didn't have the right to make that call.

"No," she insisted. "I—"

"Will need help with your goats. You might be able to walk home, but what about that little one in your back-seat?"

Common sense told her that as much as she hated to admit it, Liam was right. Leading three goats on a hike would be a challenge. Keeping the animals safe trumped the fact that she'd be forced to make the trek with him.

"I'll park my bike beside your wagon," he added, knowing he'd won. "You get your goats."

She opened the truck and picked up two lead lines designed to hook into her horses' halters. Out of the corner of her eye, she saw him shrug off his leather jacket, revealing arms toned to perfection from years of felling trees. Seven years had passed since she'd touched those muscles, and he'd only grown bigger and more imposing.

But she refused to let him cast a spell over her a second time. He wasn't the only one who'd changed, gotten stronger. Except her strength was on the inside.

"You don't have the walk the whole way. Once I get to the second turn, there is cell service. And it's only three miles to home."

"If you follow the road." Liam nodded to the wooded area to their left. "Less if we cut through there."

"No." Katie hooked the lead line around the first goat's neck. "We'll get lost."

"I know where I'm going, Katie." His voice was strong and sure. But Liam never showed weakness, except . . .

"I'm going to come."

His fingers covered hers, guiding her, showing her how to touch him.

"Now," he added, and his hand fell away. He leaned back, every muscle in his body tensing. She watched in awe as his hips thrust up, demanding more from her.

"Faster," he ordered. She obeyed, shifting her wide-eyed gaze to his face. Brown eyes open, he started back, allowing her to witness the way his climax swept over him, rendering him vulnerable, completely lost in pleasure.

In that moment, she thought he was handing over a piece of his heart. Believing he had, she gave him hers. She allowed him to take her further, teach her more. . .

Katie shut her eyes tight. It had all been an illusion. If Liam Trulane had granted her a part of himself in those moments, he'd stolen it back. And she hadn't realized until it was too late.

Back then her world had narrowed day by day,

with each kiss, until there was only Liam. She'd given him everything—her body, her love, and the ability to write her future. She'd drawn him away from his well-intentioned reasons for holding back, until they stood together in a place dominated by L-words.

At the time, she'd labeled it love. But after a month of needing, begging, and finally getting what she wanted, she'd learned in the worst possible way that it was nothing more than lust.

"Cutting through the woods will be faster than following the road," he said, pulling her away from the memories that spoke to parts of her body still craving his attention, even now after all this time—after the way things ended.

Liam walked over and took the first goat's lead, his hand brushing against hers. She pulled back as if he'd singed her skin.

His lips curled into a smile. "Trust me, Katie."

Never again.

"If you get us lost in the woods," she said, "this time I'll be the one to tell my brothers about your supposed sins."

Chapter 2

LIAM HAD A long list of transgressions—he hadn't spent the past few years living like a monk—but Katie Summers topped them all. And those sins had been very real. There was a line he knew better than to cross, but he'd blown past it anyway in one wicked night he could never take back.

And the next day, when her brothers found out about them? Well, shit, he'd screwed that up too.

He studied the way her slim hips moved beneath her sundress. With her long, graceful limbs, she looked like a model. Not that he knew much about them, having spent all of his thirty years living in rural Oregon. Though he'd bet they didn't drag reluctant livestock through the woods in freaking sandals.

Despite the goats and the rugged surroundings, Katie Summers possessed a cover girl walk, in his humble opinion, and so much more. Her bright green eyes sparkled with a silent I-dare-you. That look had drawn him in years ago and he'd accepted the challenge.

"Do you need help?" she called over her shoulder. "The little one should follow her brothers."

He tugged on the animal's makeshift lead. "I'm coming."

She raised an eyebrow, and something unreadable flashed in her eyes. He'd picked the wrong words, but with Katie he'd never been able to find the right ones.

TWENTY MINUTES LATER, Liam stepped through the brush, pulling the stubborn goat behind him into the clearing, with the baby trailing behind. Katie had charged ahead as if running from a wildfire. It helped that the goat on the end of her lead line was more compliant. And she didn't have the smallest member of the four-legged family following behind her, voicing objections every thirty seconds like a child in the backseat screaming: *Are we there yet?*

Ten paces into the clearing, Katie stopped. Liam walked to her side. Telling himself he was checking to make sure she wasn't scratched and bleeding from their hike through the overgrown forest, he examined her long, bare legs, allowing his gaze to drift north to where her short skirt met her slim thighs.

"Which way?" she demanded.

"Straight." Liam looked up from her tantalizing limbs and pointed through the field, waiting for the moment that she recognized where they were. "You should know your way home from here. This place hasn't changed much."

He watched as she took in the panoramic view of the Cascades. Her brow drew together, her head turning to the left. He knew the second she spotted the pair of fir trees in the center of the clearing. She sucked in a breath, her eyes narrowing as her hand tightened on the lead. There was no doubt about it—she knew where they were now. And she remembered every moment they'd spent together. He could see it in the way she studied the space beneath those branches.

Seven years ago, he'd met her under the twin firs nearly every day for a month. It had started with a simple picnic. He'd known her forever, grown up playing Little League with her brothers. Chad, the second eldest of the Summers brothers, had been his year in school. But that summer, Liam had been unable to resist the wild, daring gleam in Katie's eyes, or the way she'd worn her clothes shorter and tighter. Maybe it had been his imagination, or maybe she'd been pushing the limits.

She'd had a rough year. At eighteen, she'd lost her father to a sudden heart attack days after burying her grandfather. After her dad died, it was just Katie and her brothers. Her mother had walked out years earlier and never looked back.

In hindsight, he realized Katie had probably been trying to escape her grief. At the time, he just plain wanted her. So damn much that he'd put on blinders. He thought he'd found someone who wanted the same things he did. He'd pushed aside the warning signs—she was too young, too sad, and too damn innocent.

"Why did you bring me here?" she asked. There was an edge to her tone as if she didn't feel the need to hide her dislike for him when they were alone. How deep did those feeling run?

He shrugged, setting the question aside for another time and place. "Fastest way home."

"We're trespassing," she said, her gaze fixed on those trees.

"Not anymore. I bought it." He pulled on the goat's lead. He hadn't planned on revealing that fact today.

"When?"

"A few years back." *As soon as he had the money.* He'd been desperate to make this land his own.

"Why?" This time, honest wonder filled her voice.

"Nice views." He nodded to mountains visible over the tops of the distant trees. She'd grown up looking out at those peaks, but he'd always lived closer to town on a thumbprint of land in a rented home. His parents—God bless them—had gotten by on a combination of love and timber harvesting. And there had always been more love to go around than money from working in the forest, especially in the winter months.

The fear of getting kicked out of their house, of never having enough to pay the bills, had hung over his childhood. Some kids were scared of monsters under the bed. But Liam had grown up terrified of calls from collection agencies. As his dad grew older, unable to keep up in the field alongside the young guys, Liam had realized the importance of plan B—an office job that didn't require physical work, and came with health insurance.

"What are you going to do with it?" Katie asked, drawing him back to the present and the piece of land that proved he was walking down the path marked success. The equity stake in Moore Timber his best friend, Eric Moore, had offered Liam in exchange for help running the company was one more milestone on that road—and one he had yet to prove he deserved.

"Thinking about building a home here someday," Liam said.

"A house? I would have thought you'd want to forget about this place. About us. After the way you ended it." Katie raised her hand to her mouth as if she couldn't believe she'd said those words out loud.

Liam stopped beside her, losing his grip on the goat's lead and allowing the animal to graze. "I messed up, Katie. I think we both know that. But I panicked when I realized how young you were, and how—"

"I was eighteen," she snapped.

"By a few weeks. You were so innocent. And I felt all kinds of guilt for not realizing it sooner."

"Not anymore," she said, her voice firm. Defiant. "I'm not innocent anymore."

"No." Liam knew every line, every angle of her face. There were days he woke up dreaming about the soft feel of her skin. But it was the way Katie had looked at him after he'd gone too far, taken too much, that haunted his nightmares. In that moment, her green eyes had shone with hope and love.

Back then, when he was fresh out of college, returning home to build the life he'd dreamed about, that one look had sent him running scared. He wasn't ready for the weight of her emotions.

And he sure as hell wasn't ready now. Eric had given Liam one job since handing over part of the company—buy Summers Family Trucking. Liam couldn't let his best friend, now his business partner, down. Whatever lingering feelings he had for Katie needed to wait on the sidelines until after Liam finished negotiating with her brothers. There was too much at stake—including his vision of a secure future—to blow this deal over the girl who haunted his fantasies.

He drew the goat away from the overgrown grass and started toward the wooded area on the other side of the clearing. "We should go. Get you home before too late."

But Katie didn't follow. She marched down to the fir trees. "I'm twenty-five, Liam. I don't have a curfew. My brothers don't sit around waiting for me to come home."

"I know."

Brody, Chad, and Josh were waiting for him. Liam had been on his way to see her brothers when he'd spotted her car on the side of the road. They'd reluctantly agreed to an informal meeting to discuss selling to Moore Timber.

She spun to face him, hands on her hips. "I think you wanted to take a walk down memory lane."

"Katie—"

"Back then, you never held back." She closed the gap between them, the toes of her sandal-clad feet touching his boots. "So tell me, Liam, what are we doing here?"

He fought the urge to reach for her. He had no right. Not to mention bringing her here had confirmed one thing: After seven years, Katie Summers still held his mistakes against him.

She raised one hand, pressing her index finger to his chest. Damn, he wished he'd kept his leather jacket on. Her touch ignited years of flat-out need. No, he hadn't lived like a saint for seven years, but no one else turned him on like Katie Summers.

"Back then," she continued, "you asked for what you wanted."

No, he'd issued commands. He'd held nothing back—except his heart.

"Honey, if I want something," he said slowly, "you'll know."

Her eyes sparked with desire. That flash—it was unexpected, like the moment when a chainsaw blade ran up against a rock. He felt the danger, knew the warning signs. If she looked at him like that for any longer, with her full lips parted, he'd kiss her.

The baby goat pushed between them and the tension shattered. Katie stepped back, scooped up the young animal, and thrust it into his arms.

"I need you to carry the little one," she said, her tone once again hard and unforgiving. The desire he'd witnessed seconds earlier had seemingly vanished without a trace. "Her legs are tired."

He'd gone from almost kissing her to carrying her rescued goat in the blink of an eye. Whatever happened next, Katie Summers was not going to make this easy.

"Lead the way, Katie. This time, I'll follow you."

Chapter 3

KATIE TOSSED A bale of hay into the stall, watching as the goats pulled it apart. She'd placed the four-legged family in the far corner of the barn, away from her horses. She wanted them to feel safe here.

"Later, I'll bring you a bucket of grain," she told the animals. "Not that you need it. There is plenty to eat out in the fields. But I'm going to spoil you today. Tomorrow, I'll let you loose in the pasture."

Only the youngest, the little girl goat Liam had dutifully carried back to the barn, looked up from the feast.

Liam. She shook her head as she headed for the exit. After all this time, she couldn't believe she'd walked headfirst into the past. It wasn't that she avoided him. That would have proved impossible. Since Liam's little sister had returned home from serving in Afghanistan, Georgia and Katie had become close friends. In a few months, Katie would be Georgia's maid of honor when she married Eric Moore, Liam's best friend and boss. And Liam would be the best man.

No, there was no avoiding him. But that didn't mean they had to awaken old memories.

Trying to push Liam out of her thoughts, she crossed the field to the farmhouse. Her father had added a wrap-around porch, wide enough to accommodate a porch swing and a pair of rocking chairs, but otherwise the three-story structure stood much the same as it had when her grandfather first built the place. The red paint had faded and chipped in some places. A few of the wooden boards needing replacing, but they would get to that once they had a little extra money.

Katie picked up her pace. If they just held on awhile longer, they would have the money to repair the house, pay their debts, and more. She and her brothers had struggled to maintain the family business for years, but Katie had finally found a way out of their just-getting-by existence. Both Granddaddy and her father had devoted most of their lives to Summers Family Trucking, determined to leave behind a tangible legacy, and now she'd found a way to make it thrive. She just needed her brothers to trust her, to be patient, and let her finalize the details.

Glancing over at the vehicles lining the dirt and gravel parking area in front of the house Katie spotted her wagon. She'd taken her goats straight to the bar when she'd returned home, leaving Liam to beg a ride from her brothers, or wait until she finished. Seeing to the animals came first. But while she'd been busy settling the goats into their new home, her brothers had gone out, changed her tire, and driven her car home. Beside her wagon stood Liam's motorcycle.

Hands on her hips, she stared at the bike. What was he still doing here? Out of all the ten thousand or so people in Independence Falls, Liam was the last one she expected to stick around and visit with her brothers. If anyone else had come to her rescue on the side of the road, her family would offer him a drink and a game of pool. But Liam?

Every time Brody caught sight of Liam—in the grocery store, on a job site, or at the bar—fury flashed in her brother's eyes as if he was hearing Liam's words from that awful morning, seven years earlier, for the first time.

I'm so damn sorry. I'll leave her alone, I swear. You have my word that I won't touch her again. I won't go anywhere near your sister.

Katie had walked into the room that fateful morning just in time to hear Liam's apology. She'd frozen on the spot, shocked to find the man she loved, whom she had stupidly assumed loved her in return, breaking up with her—and tearing her trust to pieces in the process.

She reached the three steps leading up to the porch as the front door swung open. And there he was in his leather jacket and jeans.

"You're still here?" She glanced past him to where Chad, her middle brother, held the door. Brody and Josh stood beside him.

Her mind flashed back to the last time she'd seen Liam surrounded by her three big brothers. Brody, the oldest and most even-tempered of the three, had his arm drawn back ready to slam his fist into Liam's face. If she hadn't stepped between them, she had a feeling Brody would have thrown that punch, then another and another.

Her brothers had found out she'd been seeing Liam from one of the local gossips. When she didn't come home that night seven years ago, they had sought him out, demanding that Liam walk away from her if he wasn't serious. And Liam had. Just like that.

"He's leaving." Brody crossed his powerful arms in front of his chest. "Now."

"Katie, what the hell were you doing driving around with a flat spare?" Josh demanded. He was the youngest of her brothers, only eleven months older than she, and the only brother who'd inherited their mother's red hair and green eyes. Brody and Chad looked like twins with their dark brown hair and matching eyes.

"I didn't know."

"I'll see you around, Katie," Liam said, stopping beside her at the base of the porch steps. Out of the corner of her eye, she saw Brody step forward as if he'd personally escort Liam to his bike if he didn't keep walking. "Take care of your goats."

Liam walked away, easy and carefree, as if he hadn't spent the afternoon leading her through the past.

Brody turned his intense gaze to her. "What goats?"

Still holding the door open, Chad shook his head. "Don't tell me you brought home another stray animal, sis."

Chin held high, she marched up the steps. "I didn't have a choice. Their owner wasn't taking care of them. They deserve better."

Brody met her defiant gaze, his powerful arms crossed in front of his chest. "How many?"

"Three." She walked through the door, past Chad.

"Then you'll be glad to hear Liam offered us a way to keep your herd fed through the winter," Chad said, closing the door. He headed past the main stairs toward the large, open farm kitchen in the rear of the house, Brody and Josh behind him.

"He what?" Katie followed at her brother's heels.

"Sit down." Brody pulled out a chair and held it for her. He had crafted each piece of furniture by hand, using downed trees from their twenty acres. But that was back when her oldest brother had time to spend in his woodworking shop. Before they started saving every downed tree for firewood to heat their house or to sell to help make ends meet.

Josh claimed a seat beside the one Brody held for her while Chad headed for the fridge, pulling out a six-pack of longnecks. He set the beer on the table and went to the cupboard for a bag of chips. Chad twisted the top off one of the bottles and handed it to her before sinking into another chair.

Brody waited until everyone was settled before taking his place at the head of the table. A legal pad lined with his handwriting sat in front of him.

"Turns out Liam was on his way over when he spotted your wagon," Brody said.

Her grip tightened on her untouched beer. He'd planned to visit her brothers? The same day he'd led her past their spot under the fir trees? The day's events were like pieces of a jigsaw puzzle she couldn't fit together.

"Moore Timber wants to buy Summers Family Trucking," Chad said, cutting to the chase.

"What?" Her eyes widened and she set the bottle on the table before it slipped from her hand.

"After the snafu with B&B Trucking, Eric Moore feels his timber company would be better served by having their own trucks and drivers instead of relying on an outside vendor," Brody explained.

With four years of undergraduate business classes under her belt, that part made sense to her. "But why was Liam here and not Eric?"

She couldn't name one person in Western Oregon who didn't respect and trust Eric Moore. He'd built his late father's timber company into the largest operation in the Pacific Northwest. He had a reputation for working hard alongside his employees when needed, and he always did the right thing. He even took in his three-year-old nephew, Nate, after his sister and brother-in-law passed away in a car accident.

"It is Eric's company," she added.

"He made Liam an equity partner," Josh said. "Eric's stepping back to spend more time with Georgia and Nate. Get ready for the wedding and all."

"Seems Eric put Liam in charge of closing the deal," Chad said.

"Liam was here to buy our trucking company?" He hadn't said a word to her while they walked home. Katie bit her lower lip, her grip tightening on her beer. It wasn't as if she needed another reason to dislike Liam Trulane, but he'd given her one anyway.

"Look, I know you two have a history," Brody said.

Chad snorted.

"We didn't want that to influence your view of this deal," Josh added.

"It won't," she lied. The idea of giving control of the family business, her grandfather's baby—Summers Family Trucking—to Liam Trulane? It turned her stomach.

"But I don't think now is the right time to sell," she added.

"Look, I don't know the ins and outs of finance. Not like you do," Brody said. Of all her brothers, he was the only one who hadn't gone to college, choosing instead to stay home and run the trucking company alongside her father. But he was also the brother who understood the business side of things the best. He'd managed Summers Family Trucking for years without her help. And while Chad and Josh had graduated, they hadn't exactly focused on business management classes.

"None of us do," Chad said. "But we're not deaf. You've been saying for the past year that we're in trouble."

"We were," she clarified. "But once Mr. Fidderman at Black Hills Timber signs the contract that gives us the exclusive right haul the excess from their harvests, the limbs and other useless pieces, to the biomass plant, we're going to be fine. Better than fine. We'll make a good profit from our cut of the haul."

"Maybe," Chad said. "If he signs the contract."

"He will," Katie insisted, her attention focused on her oldest brother. "And then we won't need to sell to anyone." *Especially not Liam Trulane.*

"We can keep the business in the family. In a year or two, some of us can step back," she continued, glancing around the table at Chad and Josh, and back at Brody, whose lips formed a thin line. "If we want to do something else." She had a feeling Brody would never walk away.

"Katie," Brody said. "I want that deal to come through. But the contract with Black Hills isn't worth anything until we iron out the details. Frankly, right now all we have are a few trucks and a new chipper to process a bunch of branches no one is paying us to haul. If Mr. Fidderman doesn't come through—"

"Trust me, he will," she insisted, lifting her head. "We're just waiting for him to get back from vacation. He's going to sign."

"But there's more to this deal with Moore Timber," Josh said, setting his half-empty bottle on the table. "I never thought I'd be here. Driving trucks, hauling timber like Dad. And this is a way out."

Katie nodded. Josh's point tugged at her guarded heart. She didn't want to be here either, living at home, struggling alongside her brothers. That was why she had insisted on setting up a side business to haul biomass. She wanted to follow her dreams and find a job that allowed her to focus on doing what she loved—caring for animals. But she couldn't walk away from the business until she knew her brothers would be all right. As much as they liked to think they kept tabs on her, it ran both ways.

"If you guys really want out . . ."

Brody looked away, not meeting her gaze. Katie had a bad feeling her oldest brother was planning to sell for the wrong reasons. He'd go ahead with this deal not because he wanted out of the family business he worked night and day to run, but because he thought it was the best thing for his siblings.

That tore at her heart. After their father died suddenly, Brody had held them together. He'd set aside his own grief, and at twenty-five, her oldest brother had done his best to fill their father's shoes. And now he was willing to give it all away for them. But this time, they owed Brody, not the other way around.

"Do you want to sell, Brody?" she asked.

"I think," he said slowly, glancing at Josh, "that we should hear them out."

"OK." Katie nodded. Resting her palms flat on the smooth surface her brother had handcrafted, Katie looked around the table. "Let's say we sell and divide the profits four ways, what would you do with your share?"

"I was hoping to buy a piece of land," Josh said. "Start my own vineyard. Maybe go back to school and take some classes in viticulture."

"Land isn't cheap," she said. "Especially prime grape-growing soil."

"No." And just like that the excitement in her brother's eyes dimmed. "But I've been saving up. And picking up some logging work on the side when I can."

Still, it wouldn't be enough, and they both knew it. Unless they sold for a windfall.

Chad leaned back in his chair, lacing his fingers behind his head. "I'd buy a chopper. Start the business dad always dreamed about. A small helicopter logging company. If I'm lucky, maybe Eric Moore would hire my outfit."

Katie studied her middle brother. Behind his devil-may-care exterior, she knew that breathing life into their late father's dream was important to him. Their dad had learned to fly and maintain helicopters in the military, but then he'd come home and his wife had walked out on him. The reality of supporting a family demanded he stick with the trucking business. But that hadn't stopped him from teaching his sons to fly with lessons every week at the local airport. And Chad had fallen in love with helicopters from day one.

"You need a big, expensive chopper for logging," she said.

"I would," Chad agreed.

She turned to Brody. "And you?"

"I guess I'd spend more time volunteering with the search and rescue squad," he oldest brother said. "They're always shorthanded."

Katie frowned. "You do that now."

Brody shrugged. "I could do more."

"What about you, sis?" Josh asked. "What would you do with your share?"

She would leave behind her childhood room with the pink and purple wallpaper that was better suited to a nine-year-old girl than a twenty-five-year-old woman, and make a home for herself and her animals. A place where she could stand on her own two feet, and care for the animals others saw as worthless.

Katie picked up her beer and took a long drink. Lowering the bottle to the table, she looked at her brothers. "I'd go work at a nonprofit animal sanctuary. Maybe start my own."

She'd been working toward her goal for some time now, sending out résumés to large animal sanctuaries in surrounding states. She wouldn't go too far. She didn't want to be across the country if there was a problem with the family business. But after the Black Hills contract was in place, she trusted her brothers to handle the day-to-day.

"So you think selling is a good idea?" Josh pressed.

"No. But Brody's right. It doesn't hurt to hear their offer," she said. "Was today the first Liam mentioned the idea?"

Brody looked down at his hands. Smart man, he knew she would hate being kept in the dark. "Eric asked for the financials and I sent him the balance sheet. Today, after your little walk, Liam dropped in to ask for the profit and loss statements, that sort of thing. Can you pull that together for him? And the information on the pending contracts with Black Hills?"

Katie hesitated. "I'm not sure we should share that yet."

"We're worth a helluva lot more with it, right?" Chad said.

"We are," she replied. "But like you said, it is not final. Not yet."

And Liam Trulane was the last person she trusted with information about the pending deal.

"Eric is not exactly a fan of the biomass industry," Katie added. "He has spoken out against using the extra branches from the timber harvests to create energy."

Brody furrowed his brow. "We can't hide the information from them even if it isn't a done deal."

"She might have a point," Josh said. "I've worked with Liam and Eric's crews. Those guys believe that leaving the trees limbs to decompose on the forest floor is better for the land and the next crop of trees. They're not interested in collecting them, running them through a chipper, and selling the stuff to a biofuel plant."

Katie nodded, grateful at least one brother agreed with her. Part of her wanted to shove proof of the deal she'd negotiated in Liam's face. But she knew it made more sense to wait until the ink was dry on the contracts—and until they saw just how serious Moore Timber was about buying the Summers family business. For all she knew, Liam would take the information about the Black Hills deal and try to screw her. Again.

"I'll get the paperwork in order. If Liam didn't ask to see our pending contracts, I don't see a reason to send them," she said. "We should start thinking about a number. What we need to make the sale worthwhile. Grandpa built this company from nothing, starting with a single truck. And Daddy gave everything he had to this business."

Across the table, Brody nodded.

"We're not giving it away," she said, her voice firm. "Not to them."

Not to Liam.

"No one said we were." Brody leaned forward, resting his hands on the table. "And Katie, if you want me to talk to Eric and ask that Liam be removed from the deal, I will."

"I'm a big girl." She stood, handing off her mostly full beer to Chad. "I can negotiate with my ex-lover."

Chad closed his eyes. "Shit, Katie. If you bring that up, I might talk to Eric myself."

"Let's leave the past out of this." But as she headed for the first floor study, she wondered if that was possible.

Taking a seat behind the desk, she went to work, pulling together the information Liam requested. This would give them a place to start negotiations. And buy her some time to secure the Black Hills contract.

Her cell phone buzzed in her pocket and Katie pulled it out, glancing at the out-of-state number on the screen.

"Hello?" she said.

"Katie Summers?"

"Yes." Holding the cell with one hand, she hit print on the financial documents.

"Carol Lewis from Montana's Safe Haven for Horses," the woman said. "I apologize for calling you on a Sunday, but I've reviewed your résumé and I have an opening if you're still looking."

"Yes," Katie said quickly.

"Great," the woman on the other end of the line said. "The position is for interim director."

"Director?" Katie squeaked. "That's not possible. I mean, I'm hardly qualified."

With no experience apart from caring for her own horses and only a college degree in business that she'd never used, Katie had expected to start in an entry-level position.

"Yes," the woman said. "I've known the sheriff in your town for years. He heard I was looking for someone to run my facility for six months, maybe a year, and recommended you. He said you'd care for my horses as if they were your own. And that you're more than capable of running a business. While I need someone to step into the director's chair now, I would like to keep that person on after I return."

"I would take excellent care of your horses," she said, picturing the barns filled with animals needing a little extra love and care. "And I can handle the business side, ma'am."

"Please call me Carol. Why don't you take a couple of days to think it over and learn more about what we do here. One summer intern designed a Web site that offers an overview. I can answer any questions once you've had some time to think about whether this is what you're looking for."

"Yes." Katie squeezed her eyes shut, excitement bubbling up inside her. This was what she'd been waiting for. "I'll check out your Web site, but this job—it is exactly what I've been hoping for. More than that, really. It sounds like a dream come true."

If only the timing was better.

Chapter 4

LIAM STEPPED OVER the toy train track running through the front room of his best friend's sprawling timber frame home. "Eric? Georgia? Anybody home?"

"In here," his sister called.

He navigated around a drawbridge, heading for the archway to the kitchen. He stepped inside and found Georgia standing by the stove in her "Hug a Logger" T-shirt and jean shorts. Eric sat beside his nephew at the kitchen table, piecing together what looked like a toy dinosaur.

"Hey stranger." Georgia gave him a quick hug before returning to the stove. "Staying for dinner? Nate already ate, but after he goes to bed, Eric and I were planning to sit down for a grown-up meal."

Liam glanced over at his friend, who was no longer looking at the plastic T-rex pieces. Eric was staring at Georgia, his gaze lingering over her backside. Liam's jaw tightened. Not long ago, he'd caught Eric with his hands all over his sister. It had been a helluva way to find out his best friend and boss was sleeping with his little sister, who'd only recently returned from Afghanistan, and brought some serious baggage back with her. Liam had accepted their relationship, but he had zero interest in playing third wheel over dinner. And judging from the way Eric was watching Georgia, dinner might be delayed.

"No thanks," Liam said. "I just stopped by on my way home to fill Eric in on my meeting with the Summers brothers."

"You're still in one piece," Eric said, turning his attention back to the dinosaur. "It must have gone well."

"They didn't kick me out. Brody thought about it, but he heard me out." Liam went to the fridge and helped himself to a bottle of water. He had a feeling Brody Summers's reaction had more to do with the fact that he'd walked Katie home. "They said I'd have the rest of their financials tomorrow."

"I'll take a look at the numbers with you, but I have a feeling our starting offer will be low. I like those guys, but I don't want to overpay." Eric secured the dinosaur leg and handed the completed model to his nephew. "All done, buddy."

"Did you see Katie?" Georgia asked.

"I did." Liam leaned back against the counter.

"She told you about her potential job? The one in Montana?" Georgia stirred the pot on the stove.

Liam straightened, his hand tightening around the bottle. "No."

"A horse rescue wants to hire her. But get this. The owner is leaving for six months, maybe longer, to care for her son. He was recently diagnosed with cancer, which is awful. But Katie would be running the place while the owner was away. She'd basically have her own sanctuary."

"That's great." Liam tried to sound genuine, but the idea of Katie leaving unsettled him, more than he wanted to let on. "But I'm sorry you'll lose your friend and maid of honor."

"They haven't offered her the job yet. She still needs to do a phone interview. But she'll get the position. When she accepts, I will make her promise to return for the wedding," Georgia said. "I'll miss her, but Katie has been counting down the days until she can focus on doing what she loves. And I get the feeling she is ready to leave the watchful eyes of her older brothers."

"Big brothers can be a pain in the—"

"Language," Georgia warned him, waving her wooden spoon at the little boy playing with his dinosaur.

"Sorry." Liam crossed to the stove and gave his sister a quick kiss on the cheek. "I should get going. Long day. Eric, I'll see you at the office."

In the driveway, Liam sat on his bike, engine off, staring out at the mountains. The land he'd bought and planned to build on one day had a similar view. But somewhere between her broken-down car and the long walk to the barn cradling her goat, he'd realized that he couldn't shake the memory of Katie. He'd never forget her. Worse—he'd never stop wanting her. And this time he needed more than stolen moments in parking lots.

But he couldn't go after her now. Not with the deal undone. But if he didn't act soon, she would leave.

"Freaking Montana," he muttered, closing his eyes, blocking out the view. His road to success suddenly felt like it might take a detour to failure.

Liam opened his eyes and focused on his bike, revving the engine. He couldn't afford to make a wrong turn and end up like his dad. Still, something inside him refused to accept the thought of Katie walking out of his life.

TWENTY-FOUR HOURS LATER, Liam stood in the gas station waiting for the attendant to fill up the fifty-gallon drum he kept in the back of his truck. It was there just in case his crew ran out of gas to run the chainsaws out in the forest. Today had been one of those days. But shit, it was Monday, which probably explained why anything that could go wrong on a job site had gone wrong.

Hands on his hips, he hoped the attendant would hurry up. Liam had been working since before dawn and his body ached from head to toe. He needed a shower and then bed. But first he had to review the financials Brody had dropped off that morning and send Eric his thoughts on a starting offer.

Shaking his head, Liam turned and headed for the station to pick up a coffee. He needed something to keep him up tonight and—

"Liam!"

The familiar voice that up until, oh, *now*, only screamed his name in his dreams, called for him a second time. He glanced over his shoulder and spotted Katie. She'd traded her short skirt for jeans and a T-shirt, but with her red curls flowing over her shoulders and her determined walk, she looked pretty damn enticing.

He smiled as he ran a hand through his dirty hair even though nothing short of a shower would make it presentable. "Hey, how are the goats?"

"Fine." She stopped an arm's length away. "But they were as surprised as I was to learn we hiked through the woods and you never bothered to mention that you were looking at buying my family's trucking company."

He raised an eyebrow. "You talk business with your livestock?"

"When it concerns how I'm planning to earn money to buy their grain, yes."

"Fair point." Liam stared into her green eyes, shinning bright. Right now, he was too damn tired for this conversation. And he had a feeling the Independence Falls gas station wasn't the place. "But it didn't come up."

Her eyes widened. "Didn't come up? Seriously? That's your excuse?"

He drew a deep breath. "Look, Katie, at the time, getting you home safe seemed more important than a deal that may or may not happen."

It better damn well go through, he thought. He refused to fail his first task as an equity partner. The last thing he wanted was Eric kicking him out of the offices. He might feel out of place there now, but he had a feeling one day soon—like ,oh, say, today—sitting in a chair might sound a lot more appealing than felling trees.

She crossed her arms in front of her chest, forcing her breasts to swell over the edge of her fitted scoop neck T-shirt. Right now, he was just tired enough to get caught staring if he wasn't careful. He lifted his gaze to her face.

"But if you want to discuss the deal," he continued, knowing he needed to get out of there before his eyes—and his thoughts—wandered. "I'm game for dinner."

"Dinner?" she repeated, her green eyes widening.

"I'm not in the office much and I'd have a hard time hearing you on a job site," he said. "So yeah, dinner."

Years ago, they'd spent a lot of time together, but he'd never taken her on a formal date. He'd been so focused on being alone with her that it had never occurred to him. But this time, if he was going after her, he had to do it right.

He knew he should wait. Take her out after the deal closed and not under the pretense of a business meeting. But that one word—Montana—echoed in his head. He'd already let seven long years slip by. He'd always had an excuse. She was too young. She'd never forgive him for how things ended. And when he went after her, he wanted to have more, to prove he deserved a place in her life.

But now he owned land and a stake in Moore Timber, one he hoped like hell he could keep. He couldn't afford to wait any longer. If he did, she'd be long gone.

"What do you say?" he asked, pressing the issue at hand—dinner.

"No."

"I'd hate for you to feel left out of the discussion."

Katie turned and headed for her car. "We don't need

to share a meal to fix that, Liam. You just need to try talking to me instead of my brothers."

Liam watched her walk away, his resolve hardening with each step. If he didn't go after her soon, she'd climb into her car and go a helluva lot farther than the Summers farm. Dinner was a solid first step. After last time, he couldn't push for too much too fast. But first he had to convince her to say yes.

KATIE RAN THE brush over Sugar, the gentle mare she'd rescued from a family who could no longer afford the feed bills during the winter months. The horse had been skin and bones back then, but now her coat shone and her belly had filled out. As she ran her hand down the horse's neck, her mind jumped from the sale to Montana to . . . Liam.

She paused, resting her forehead against the mare's smooth neck. "I have important life-changing decisions to make, choices that affect my family and my future," she murmured. "And I'm thinking about dinner with a boy."

Sugar let out a soft neigh.

"You're right," Katie said with a sigh, lifting her head. "He's not a boy. He's a walking, talking fantasy on a motorcycle."

And a heartbreaker. She couldn't forget that. He was still the same Liam Trulane who'd walked away when her brothers demanded to know if he was serious about her, if he cared for her—

"Hey sis," Chad said from the door to the trucking

company office, housed in the front of the barn. "Brody wants us back at the house. Liam called. We have an offer."

"Wait a minute and I'll walk up with you." She unsnapped the cross ties from Sugar's halter and led the mare back to her stall. Minutes later, she followed her brother to the main house.

Brody sat at the kitchen table and the siblings quickly took their places.

"What's the number?" Chad asked. "What are we worth?"

Her brother's mouth formed a grim line. "According to Moore Timber, one million dollars."

Katie felt her anger simmer, quickly turning to a boil. She'd expected a low initial offer. Still, a million? It sounded like a fortune, but she knew better.

"The trucks alone are worth more than that," she said. "Each one would sell for about two hundred thousand."

"Maybe," Brody said. "Some are getting old."

"A million dollars isn't enough," she insisted. "Factor in taxes, and the debt we need to pay off on the new equipment, and we're left with less than half that after the sale. Then divide it four ways and we each walk away with a hundred thousand if we're lucky."

"So what do you suggest we do?" Josh cut in. "Tell them hell no?"

"We come up with a counteroffer. Buy some more time," she said.

"Any idea when your friend at Black Hills plans to sign those contracts?" Brody asked.

"I'm meeting with Mr. Fidderman on Thursday," she said.

"We can't afford to blow this," Brody said slowly. "It's not like companies are lining up to buy the business. I think we should tell Liam about the potential deal. They probably already saw the recently purchased tractor-trailers and the chipper on the inventory."

"Not yet," Katie shot back. Why was it so hard for her brothers to trust her? They let her manage the bookkeeping, but when it came to the big decisions, it was as if they turned a blind eye to the fact that she had studied finance and been on track to go to business school. Then Eric Moore, and his new equity partner Liam Trulane, entered the picture and they started second-guessing her.

"Katie," Brody said. "There's a chance this thing with Black Hills isn't worth as much as you think. If that's the case, we need to do what is best for the company."

Katie ground her teeth. "It is also possible Liam would ruin the deal. This offer, it could all be a scheme to ruin our negotiations with Moore Timber's leading competitor."

"I don't like Liam either, but I don't think he would do something like that," Brody said. "This might be the best offer we'll get. And the timing . . . Katie, I want you to take that job if the woman in Montana offers it."

Katie closed her eyes. She hated hearing the defeated note in her big brother's voice. And the thought of leaving Brody without the business he'd fought to hold on to? In exchange for so little?

"Maybe we should put this to a vote?" Josh offered.

Katie opened her eyes, glancing around the table and

confirming her suspicions. Her brothers were willing to take the deal. She could see it in their expressions. Well, maybe not Chad. He appeared to be on the fence. But Josh wanted out. And Brody would put everyone else's wishes first.

"We're worth more," she said. "I know we are. Let's put together a counteroffer. And then as soon as the contract with Black Hills is finalized, we can make the call. But please, let's not do it because we feel trapped. We're not."

"I'm willing to see if they'll bump up the price," Brody said. "But make it reasonable. We don't want to drag this out. Not with you moving to Montana."

"I might not get the job," she said.

"You will," Brody insisted.

Katie smiled. "Thanks for the vote of confidence, but I still need to ace the interview. Until then, I'll be drafting our response to Moore Timber."

Katie stood and headed for the study. Inside, she shut the door and leaned back against the solid wood surface. Last week, finding a location for Georgia's bachelorette had felt like the most pressing issue. But now? She had to keep her oldest brother from sacrificing everything, make certain Black Hills signed, and deal with the man who'd broken her heart.

Liam.

Had he known when he asked her to dinner that he planned to toss out a lowball offer? Running into her on the side of the road had not felt premeditated. Neither had the gas station. But Liam Trulane had tricked her before.

"I'm not some inexperienced little girl anymore," she whispered to the empty room. She wasn't going to let Liam mess with her future. No, she'd given him power over her once. She'd do anything to prevent that from happening again.

"I still can't believe they let him in the front door," she muttered as she went over to the desk and sat down, her hands moving over the keys as she opened the documents and started drafting their counteroffer. She paused and stared at the screen. The number was too low. She deleted it and started typing again. "I spend one night with him and they threaten him. But when he comes after our business, they don't chase him away."

Her hands stilled on the keys. What if her brothers found out Liam was coming after her again? If she said yes to Liam's dinner invitation, and maybe more, word would get back to her brothers. What if she took it a step further, and this time, she seduced him?

The plan forming in her mind had revenge written all over it. But part of her wanted to be the one who walked away this time. And she couldn't help feeling as if Liam deserved it.

It would have been one thing if he'd come to her seven years ago and ended their fling. She would have been just as heartbroken. And she would have felt just as stupid for believing that one night with him meant he loved her. But it would have spared her the humiliation of facing her brothers—and finding out from them that what she'd thought of as special had amounted to nothing more than down-and-dirty fucking.

She squeezed her eyes shut at the memory. A soft knock on the study door drew her back to the present.

"Katie?" Chad poked his head in. "Can I come in?"

"Sure."

Her brother sank into the armchair across from the desk. Chad looked out of place with his torn jeans and grease-stained T-shirt. Of course, it was only late afternoon. In a few hours, once he'd showered and changed, he'd present a very different side of the hardworking truck driver to the women at the bar in town. She suspected that of all her brothers, Chad used the apartment over the barn—the only bedroom removed from the house, the one they were supposed to save for visiting guests—the most.

"I just wanted to let you know that if it comes to a vote, I'm on your side. I want to make enough from the sale for a down payment on a chopper." Her brother, who was seldom serious, appeared lost in sentiment. "I don't want to give up the business unless I can make Dad's dream a reality. Flying helicopters was his first love, but he set it aside to keep the trucking company, to support us. And I'm with you, I don't want to give it away."

"We're not going to," Katie said firmly. "I have a plan. I'm going to talk to Liam."

Chad leaned forward in his chair, resting his elbows on his knees. "If he tries anything, you tell me, OK?"

"I'm a big girl," Katie said.

"I know." Her brother flashed the smile that roped women in. "But I'm bigger."

"I promise to call if I need you," she said, feeling a

tinge of guilt at using her brother's protective instincts to kill their deal. But their family had worked too hard for too long to settle.

Chad pushed to his feet and headed for the door. "I'm going into town tonight. You?"

"Not sure yet." It all depended on Liam.

He nodded. "All right. Don't work too late, sis."

She waited until he closed the door. Once the sound of his boots on the hardwood floors faded, she pulled out her cell and dialed. "Liam? It's Katie."

"Hi," he said, and she heard the roar of machinery in the background. "Give me a second to move someplace quiet."

She waited, listening as the sounds of the work site faded.

"Katie," he said. "What can I do for you?"

"I'd like to accept your invitation to dinner," she said, hoping she wasn't making a huge mistake. "To talk business."

"That's . . . wow, that's great. How's tonight?" he asked. In the background, she could hear someone calling his name. "Six o'clock?"

"Fine," she said. "I'll meet you at your place."

He hesitated. "Your brothers don't know?"

"No," she said. "And we're not telling them."

"Works for me, honey."

I'm not your "honey." She bit back the words, quickly ending the call. It was time for Liam to realize he wasn't the only one who could call the shots.

Chapter 5

LIAM LEANED AGAINST his bike trying not to feel like a freaking teenage girl waiting for a prom date. But he couldn't stop staring at the road, waiting for a sign of Katie's wagon. He glanced at his watch. Two minutes past. Had she changed her mind?

Shaking his head, he turned back to the house. He felt like a fool, freshly showered and shaved, wearing his only pair of jeans that weren't shredded down at the bottom from catching on trees. He'd even thought about stopping by Eric's place and borrowing one of his friend's fancy button-down shirts.

But this was just a business dinner at the Ale House by the lake. *If* she ever showed.

Maybe this was Katie's idea of payback. Hell, he couldn't blame her. Looking back, he knew he deserved to be stood up, and a helluva lot more.

Katie's beat-up wagon rounded the bend and turned

into his driveway, pulling up alongside his motorcycle. She climbed out and walked around the car.

"Sorry I'm late. One of the goats got his head stuck in the fence," she said.

"No problem. I'm glad you're here. Hell, I was surprised you said yes in the first place."

"Well, I was downright shocked by your offer."

Liam chuckled. "So that's what this is about. That number was just a place to start the conversation, and I think you know it."

"You'll have our response in the morning," she shot back.

"Fair enough." He cocked his head. "Still joining me for dinner?"

"I am." She slipped her hands into the front pockets of her jeans. On her feet, she wore black cowboy boots, and on top, a fitted tank that hugged her curves—or what he could see of them beneath her jean jacket. He was dying to slip his hands under there and explore.

"But there is no way, I'm climbing on the back of that thing," she added, nodding to his bike.

He raised an eyebrow, his lips forming a smile. He liked how she didn't hold her punches. "It's a lot more fun than riding in your chewed-up wagon."

"I heard you kept your bike locked up all summer. How can I trust you'll get us there in one piece?" She adjusted the thin black leather strap holding her purse. It ran from one shoulder to the opposite hip. He wanted to reach out, slip his fingers under the leather, and draw her close. But he couldn't. Not yet.

"Katie, I'm still as good as I ever was on this bike." He picked up the spare helmet resting on his motorcycle and held it out to her. "I kept it in storage because I didn't want Georgia to get any ideas in her head about taking it for a joyride back when she was hell-bent on seeking one adventure after another."

Katie stared at him for a minute, before relenting. She took the helmet, positioning it between her knees as she reached back and pulled her hair into a ponytail. Tonight, her naturally curly red hair hung long and straight.

"Georgia scared you, didn't she?" she said.

He nodded. "Mostly because I didn't know how to help her. She came back from the army with a laundry list of fears and nightmares that left her fighting to stay awake day and night."

No matter how long he lived, he'd never forget the sound of his sister's screams when she'd been lost in the throes of a nightmare. He'd wanted to erase her pain, her memories, anything to stop the nightmares. But he couldn't. As much as he wanted to sometimes, he couldn't change the past.

"Is she sleeping now?" Katie asked.

"Some. I think having Eric around helps."

"They're good for each other."

"They are." It had taken him a while to face that fact, but he had. "You changed your hair."

"I used a blow dryer." She held the helmet up, but paused before pulling it on. "Mind telling me where we're going?"

"The Ale House," he said.

"I thought you'd prefer someplace private." Her green eyes flashed with the challenge he remembered from years ago.

"Trust me, honey, I'll enjoy having you on the back of my bike for the next forty-five minutes. But if we're talking business, a restaurant outside of Independence Falls seemed like the best place." He straddled the motorcycle, rocking it off the kickstand. "Ready to climb on?"

Placing her hands on his shoulders, Katie slid onto the back of his bike. She positioned her feet and wrapped her arms around his waist. He could feel her breasts pressed up against his back as he revved the engine. Her thighs touched his—and shit, he wasn't sure he'd survive nearly an hour of full body contact knowing that tonight wouldn't end with Katie naked in his arms. But he couldn't go there yet. He had to wait until the deal closed.

Needing to calm his body's reaction to the close contact, Liam mentally recited the Latin names for trees native to this part of Western Oregon as he steered the bike onto the road and headed for the highway.

KATIE HAD A long list of weapons in her arsenal, but none she could deploy on the Ale House's crowded back porch overlooking the lake. She'd planned to seduce him, using her body, playing on his desires. But the public location, coupled with the motorcycle ride, had her at a disadvantage.

Her body hummed from head to toe as if she'd been pressed up against a vibrator without hope of release while her hands clung to Liam's hard, sculpted body. Those muscles toned to perfection from felling trees and wielding chainsaws, made her mouth water and left her aching. Right now, she wanted to pull him into a quiet corner, strip away his clothes, and enjoy every inch of him.

But if she let go of her anger, if she gave in to desire, she had a bad feeling all she would be left with was hurt. It would be like ripping off the Band-Aid covering a wound that had yet to heal.

She studied Liam out of the corner of her eye as the waiter set down her beer and his soda. They placed their orders—a veggie burger for her and a bison one for him. Liam added an order of the spinach/artichoke dip to start.

"Spinach, huh?" she said.

"Bacon-wrapped scallops were my first choice, but seeing as you're the only woman I know who doesn't enjoy bacon, I went with the dip," he said.

"You remembered." And her mind, still distracted from their ride, wondered what other facts he'd stored away.

"That you're a vegetarian? Yeah, I remember. I'm not saying I approve. No one should bypass bacon," he teased. "Even Georgia thinks it is a sin."

She arched an eyebrow. "Have you told Georgia about this?"

"That I'm taking you to dinner?" He raised his soft drink to his lips. "No."

"And Eric?"

"I didn't see him today," Liam said. "I was out on a job

site harvesting a tract of land for Wilson's widow. Your brothers agreed to haul the logs to the mill tomorrow."

She crossed her legs, allowing her jeans-clad calf to brush up against his under the table. It was time to reach into the arsenal and deploy her weapons. She watched as his eyes widened in surprise. "Spent all day running your chainsaw?"

"No." He set his glass back on the wooden tabletop, but kept his leg firmly pressed against hers. "I was operating the mechanical timber harvester. The land over there is flat. No need to have guys out there cutting with chainsaws."

"You sat all day, pushing levers?" She shook her head, raising her beer to her lips and taking a sip—and felt his gaze drop to her mouth. "Well, that ruins the image of the tall, dark, and handsome lumberjack wielding dangerous machinery, doesn't it?"

His eyes narrowed and he reached across the table. Claiming her hand, he turned it over and ran his thumb across her palm. Her breath caught. Maybe she wasn't the only one who could play this game.

"Katie, if it makes you happy, I was running chainsaws from the moment I set foot on the job site."

"Hmm," she murmured, feeling his light, teasing touch from head to toe. "Without a shirt?"

He leaned back in his chair, withdrawing his hand as he let out a low laugh. "Not a chance, honey. Not a chance."

The waiter interrupted, placing the spinach/artichoke dip on the table between them. Katie shifted in her seat, breaking contact with him. Looking at this man, she couldn't picture him behind a desk, pushing papers and reviewing financials. "Do you miss being out there every day? In the forest?"

He shrugged. "Most days I still am."

Her brow furrowed. "I thought Eric wanted you to take a larger role in the business side of things."

"That's part of the deal," he said. "And I'll tell you one thing, if all business dinners are like this one, I should have moved into the office a long time ago."

"Doubtful." She suspected that most of the men negotiating deals with Moore Timber had zero interest in seducing Liam. She dipped a cracker into the steaming dish.

"I'm curious," she continued. The question of why he was here, why he'd tossed out a low offer now, when she was on the verge of closing the deal with Black Hills, was ever-present in her mind. "If your first love is working in the field, why did you agree to spend time in the office? Negotiating acquisitions doesn't seem like your thing."

Liam glanced out at the water. "I don't want to follow in my father's footsteps and work in the forest until the end. That land we walked through the other day?"

She nodded, picturing the trees and the things they'd done below them. She tried to push the thoughts away, but the memories refused to budge. Shifting in her seat, her thighs rubbed together and she drew her lower lip between her teeth.

Liam chuckled. "You remember."

But then his expression turned serious. "I want to build my own place on that land. Make a home, something nice.

You probably didn't notice when we walked through with the goats, but I've already started thinning the surrounding forest. When I'm done, it will look like a park.

"But it's about more than just the land," he added. "I want my kids to have a future and choices—beyond logging or joining the military."

"Wow." She didn't have another word. The Liam she'd known, the man she'd met out in that field, he hadn't looked much beyond one night of pleasure.

But that was before he lost his parents to cancer. Before his sister graduated college and joined the army. Before he waited day and night for Georgia to come back, knowing he couldn't keep her safe. Katie had a feeling that Georgia's choice had a ripple effect, one that continued even now that she was home.

"Georgia could have done anything with her life," he said quietly. "But for reasons I still don't fully understand, she joined the army. If I'd had something more to offer her here, a way for her to continue in school . . ."

"She would have gone anyway," Katie said. "Georgia wanted to make her way in the world."

"Yeah. I know." He polished off the last of the dip.

"But you hate losing control."

Liam studied her, not saying a word as the server removed the dip and set down their burgers. "You remember that too, huh?"

"I was angry with you for a long time, Liam," she said. "But I never wanted to forget that night."

And even if she wanted to, she couldn't escape those memories.

"Are you still?" he asked, picking up his burger. "I know your brothers hold a grudge. It was written all over Brody's face when I stopped by. But do you?"

"No. It was a long time ago." And that was a big, fat lie. She wouldn't be here if she didn't. But this time, it was about more than a grudge. She wanted payback for the way he'd hurt her—and she wanted him to stay far, far away from Summers Family Trucking.

"When I think about you," she said softly, leaning closer, "I don't envision friendly dinners in crowded places. You were always an orgasm-first, talk-second kind of guy."

He raised an eyebrow as he set his burger down and wiped his mouth. "Maybe I'm turning over a new leaf."

"What if I liked the bad boy who spent his days working with his hands in the woods, and his nights getting down and dirty under the stars?"

Heat flared in his eyes. That look promised wicked things. "I haven't changed that much. But I'd like to wine and dine you first. And talk."

"About?"

"Whatever you want."

"And then?" she challenged.

"You want me to spell it out?" His voice was a low rumble.

She nodded and her pulse sped up. Her body was hovering precariously close to needing things from him. Naughty touches, stolen kisses, and so much more, as if it hadn't gotten the memo that this was an act, a show put on to trick Liam.

"Do you see that cabin over there?" Liam leaned back in his chair and pointed at the lake.

She glanced over her shoulder. "Which one?"

"You might need to come over here for a better view." He pushed back from the table and patted his lap.

"I've seen a cabin before, Liam."

"Humor me."

Katie rose and moved to his side of the wooden table. Bending over, she offered him a view down her tank top. Liam took the bait and stared, his jaw tightening. While she'd grown wiser since the last time he had stolen a peek down her shirt, her breasts hadn't changed one bit. She'd always been on the small side. But back then, he'd labeled them perfect and given her every reason to believe him.

Without warning, he looped an arm around her waist, drawing her down to his lap. The hard ridge of his erection pressed against her bottom.

She shifted her hips, rocking against him, letting him know she hadn't missed the evidence that he was turned on. "I get the feeling you'd rather be somewhere else," she murmured.

"We'll get there." His lips brushed her ear as he spoke, keeping his voice low. "And when we do . . ."

He nipped her ear and Katie closed her eyes, feeling his palm flat against her belly. "I promise to take my shirt off for you."

His thumb brushed the underside of her bra. Her breasts would barely fill his hands. She knew that for a fact. But every inch of skin covered by her lace underwear was super sensitive. She bit back a long, low moan, knowing that if he touched her again, even through the barrier of her clothes, she wouldn't be able to keep quiet.

"What next?" she demanded, opening her eyes and focusing on his words. "After you take off your shirt?"

He let out a low chuckle. "How about I start before I undress?"

"No." She ran her hand up his leg, wanting to touch him anywhere she could reach from her forward-facing position on his lap.

"Oh yes, honey." His free hand captured her wrist, holding tight, preventing her from wandering and exploring.

"First, I'd strip off your clothes," he continued, his voice a low growl. "I'm dying to see every inch of you. Touch you. Taste you. And make you scream. I want to hear my name on your lips over and over."

"Liam," she gasped. The way he held, preventing her from touching him, pushed against the limits of her self-control.

"And I bet that cabin over there has a bed," he continued. "Some of my wildest fantasies involve lying you down on top of soft sheets, licking you from head to toe."

"Fantasies?" she repeated. That one word pulled her out of the teasing game. Her reasons for saying yes to dinner had everything to do with the deal to buy her family's company. And his? She'd suspected he was targeting her as a way to get to her brothers, mistakenly believing she was the weakest link, a way to learn more about pending contracts and unsigned deals. But if he'd been dreaming about her . . .

He released her wrist and his hand captured hers, interlacing their fingers. "This time," he whispered, "I'll be soft and sweet."

As she stared at the calm surface of the lake and the cabin in the distance, images of moments she'd never forget flashed before her.

Her hands held behind her back, not because he'd bound them together, but because he'd told her to keep them there . . . the feel of Liam taking her as if he couldn't wait, as if he needed to make her his. . .

She didn't want soft and sweet from Liam. Not then and not now. "Trying to make amends for the past?" she asked.

"I want to give you new memories." He nipped her ear.

Oh God, she was going to melt into a puddle of take-me-now desire if he did that again. "And if I like the old ones?"

"We'll get there too," he said.

"Umm, sorry to interrupt," the waiter said.

Katie jolted upright on Liam's lap, feeling her face heat. If she had a mirror, she knew she would see bright red cheeks staring back at her. Her bottom still pressed against Liam's lap, she glanced at the young man, probably close to her age, holding a second set of menus.

"Can I interest you in dessert?" the waiter added.

Liam squeezed her hand. "What do you say? Still hungry?"

"They don't have what I want on the menu." Slowly,

she rose from Liam's lap and walked past the wide-eyed waiter to her side of the table.

"Just a check," Liam said. "We need to hit the road."

Katie sank into her chair. The motorcycle. An hour with her body pressed up against his, the large machine vibrating beneath her. How was she going to survive the ride home? She stared at the man across the table. She wasn't. Not without a kiss, a touch—maybe even an orgasm right here in the Ale House parking lot.

LIAM TOOK HER hand, leading her through the maze of parked cars and pickups to his bike. He needed to get her back to Independence Falls and safely seated in her wagon, heading home to her brothers. His jaw set, his teeth grinding together, he held on to that plan. He was determined to do this right, damn it. When they got down and dirty, there would be nothing holding them back. She would know that she was *his*.

Now wasn't the time and place. She'd asked if he was trying to make amends for the past, and in a way, he was. He'd been too stupid and afraid to fall for her back then. He wouldn't repeat that mistake.

Moving too quickly, taking the fleeting pleasure she offered over a supposed business dinner, would only lead to a dead end. He'd traveled that road, and the sign where the pavement ended? It read "FAILURE" in big red letters. And that wasn't an option for him.

He stopped beside his bike, quickly handed her the

spare helmet, and threw one leg over his ride. Hell, his jeans were too tight. And having her holding on to him for the next hour would be hell. When he got home, he was headed straight for a cold shower. Alone.

Liam sat upright, hoping she wouldn't notice that he'd left the restaurant still at half-mast. Before he could stop her, Katie put her foot over his, sliding her leg across his lap. That bold move had him reaching for her. It didn't matter that they were in a parking lot, the sun still peeking over the coastal ranger. Katie Summers stirred something inside him. Knowing he should end their evening with a simple kiss didn't change his desire to take more. Perched on the front of his bike, the handlebars at her back, she pressed up against him.

"Now how am I supposed to drive like this?" he murmured, his hands gliding up her slim waist, teasing the breasts he was dying to touch and taste.

She inched closer. Her fingers brushed the nape of his neck, working their way up to his hair. "You're not."

"Katie." He heard the hint of desperation in his voice.

She touched her mouth to his skin, running her lips, her teeth, her tongue, over his jawline. Liam closed his eyes. Now would be a damn good time to stop, but he couldn't do it. She drew her body flush against him, rising up until her breath brushed against his ear.

"My turn," she said, her voice low and heavy with need. "If I took you to that cabin, I'd give you a night you would never forget. I would tease you until you begged. This time, I want you screaming *my* name, begging *me* for more. After all that, if you're ready for round two in the bed, you'd better be ready and willing to bind me to the bedposts."

His pulse raced at the image of Katie tied to his bed. He wanted that and so much more.

"I remember what turns you on. What makes you lose control," she added, running her hand down his chest, pressing her palm against his erection. "And I liked it."

He grabbed her wrist and drew her teasing fingers away from his crotch before he came on his damn bike. "Katie," he growled. "We're in a parking lot."

"I know. And I'll play by your rules." She shifted back willingly, allowing him to see the wicked gleam in her green eyes. "I'll wait until you're ready to give me everything. No holding back."

Liam closed his eyes. He felt her slide off the bike and move to the rear seat. He'd never held back. Not with her. But letting her in, showing her what he wanted, that was his biggest regret.

"I need to take you back to your car. Now," he said, his voice low and rough. Opening his eyes, he glanced over his shoulder. "Put your helmet on."

She smiled. "I always liked it when you made demands."

"Katie," he said, facing forward. "I think I liked you better with curly hair."

He revved the bike knowing that was a lie. He liked Katie Summers just the way she was and always had.

Chapter 6

KATIE WIGGLED HER freshly painted toes. The pink paint sparkled in the sunlight. She had a mountain of paperwork waiting for her, but Georgia had called and suggested that they meet at the nail salon to talk while Nate was at preschool. Liam's little sister might have shifted roles from former soldier working as a live-in nanny to fiancée, but she had no intention of finding a new caregiver for the three-year-old. Katie had to admire her friend's steadfast dedication to a child who'd lost his parents.

The back door to Ariel's Salon slammed. Katie spotted Georgia slowly making her way to the backyard nail drying area, a glass of lemon water in one hand and a notebook in the other. She claimed a seat on the bench beside Katie, facing the stunning view of the distant mountains.

"You know, this place is pretty," Katie said. "I bet Ariel

would let us have your bachelorette party here. We could bring in the champagne, have some girl time."

Georgia shook her head, her brown hair falling into her face. "After touring through the vineyards, I've decided I want something more daring."

"We're not doing anything that involves jumping out of a plane." Katie knew her friend had returned home from Afghanistan with a burning desire to live her life to the fullest, but Georgia had calmed down since she had fallen in love with Eric—or at least she'd stopped her wild, risky stunts.

"Eric said the same thing. But there is a difference between skydiving and wine tasting. I went online and made a list." Georgia opened her notebook and withdrew a sheet of paper.

Katie scanned the five potential party venues. "A country bar with a mechanical bull? Is there one in town?"

"Not in Independence Falls. But there must be one nearby. I also added nightclub to the list. Number two. Eric's afraid it will be too crowded for me. I'm still having a hard time with large groups of people. But I'd love to go dancing again."

Hearing the wistful note in Georgia's voice, Katie made a mental note to include dancing in their plans. "We don't have to go to a nightclub for that."

"True," Georgia said. "And we might have to knock clubbing off the list unless we can find one that allows dogs."

Katie looked up from the paper. "Why are we bringing a dog with us?"

"It wouldn't be much of a party with just you and me. And I don't have a lot of girlfriends left in Independence Falls. So I invited Lena. She's in my veterans' therapy group, the one that gets together each week in Portland. She is the only other woman who is about our age. I don't know her well, but I get the sense she's been struggling to reconnect with her friends. Recently Lena received a service dog trained to help with her PTSD. Wherever Lena goes, the dog goes."

Katie nodded. This was Georgia's party. If she wanted to bring dogs, they would find a way to make it possible.

"I'm eliminating the sleepover at Eric's beachfront condo," Katie said. "It will be too cold in a few months to go to the coast and swim in the ocean, even in wetsuits."

"Which brings us back to dancing all night or numbers four and five," Georgia said.

Katie tried to picture their merry group—one former soldier recently returned from the Middle East, a second woman with PTSD, a service dog, and herself—at a nightclub. That plan had disaster written all over it.

"First, we need to expand the guest list. I'll come up with a few names. Add some friends from high school who are still in town."

Georgia nodded. "OK."

"And I'll look into four and five," Katie promised, scanning the list. "Wait, what is a boudoir photo shoot?"

Georgia's eyes lit up. "I read about this online. They recommended using a hotel suite, but I thought maybe we could add our own twist. Rent a cabin in the woods by the lake and do the photo shoot there."

Katie heard the word "cabin" and thought of Liam, whispering in her ear the things he wanted to do to her. How could he infuriate her and turn her on at the same time? It didn't seem fair. But when it came to Liam Trulane, fair wasn't part of the picture.

"The photographer comes to our selected location," Georgia continued. "He said we can wear as much or as little as we want, and afterward we each have a collection of intimate pictures to share with whomever we want."

"I think your fiancé might have some objections," Katie said. "Starting with the fact the person taking the pictures is a he."

"Eric might love the final product." Georgia studied her toes. "We could do the girls' getaway at the cabin without the photographer, I guess. But this sounded fun and different. A twist to the traditional hiking and camping routine."

"I'll look into it." But talking about cabins—and thinking of Liam—she knew she had to tell Georgia about last night.

"I had dinner with your brother."

Georgia's eyebrows shot up. "Really? Just dinner, or did you stay for a sleepover?"

"It was a business dinner. Sort of. I went home." After that kiss on his bike . . .

"I love my brother," Georgia said. "But he's not exactly boyfriend material. You know that, right? I can't recall his last serious relationship."

"I'm not looking for long-term. Not here in Independence Falls."

"You're taking the job?"

"I haven't received an offer yet," Katie said. "My interview is set for Thursday."

"They'll make an offer. And you should take it."

"My brothers said the same thing. And I want to say yes, but it's complicated. Now doesn't feel like the right time to leave."

Georgia raised an eyebrow. "Because of my brother?"

"No." Katie shook her head. "*No.* I'm not interested in a relationship with Liam."

"Does that have anything to do with the fact that your brothers don't like him very much?"

"Maybe a little."

Georgia nodded. "Now that he is negotiating the deal for your company, things could get complicated."

"They already are." She wasn't about to tell Georgia her plan to seduce Liam and send the small-town rumor mill into a frenzy that would inevitably make its way back to her brothers. But the history? She had a feeling that would rise to the surface soon. "We had a fling. Liam and I."

Georgia shifted on the bench, turning to face her. "When? While I was deployed?"

"Before that. The summer before I went to college. You'd already left for school."

"Let me guess, it ended when your brothers found out and started throwing punches."

"That was part of it." Betrayal, coupled with the way he'd taken her love and handed it back to her, ended things.

"Are you going to see him again?" Georgia asked.

"Yes. But whatever happens, however it ends—" Given her plan, she knew it wouldn't end well. "I hope it doesn't change our friendship."

"As long as you two are still speaking when it comes time to stand up at our wedding, we'll be fine."

Katie nodded. But she had a feeling that in a few days, Liam Trulane would have every reason to never say another word to her.

FOUR MILLION DOLLARS.

Liam stared at the paper the receptionist had handed him. Brody Summers had dropped off their counteroffer while Liam had been out on a job site. But Liam didn't have the first clue what to make of that number. He'd known their initial bid was low, but to counter with freaking four million dollars?

He walked past the closed door to his own bare office and stood at Eric's door. Knocking once, he waited for Eric to call him in—just in case Georgia had stopped by.

"Just the man I wanted to see." Eric stood and went to the mini-fridge in the corner of his office. "Georgia pushed up the date of the wedding. She's thinking Valentine's Day. Claims she doesn't want to wait until spring."

"A holiday wedding, huh?"

"I'd marry her tomorrow, but she wants to do this right. I spent my morning looking at wedding venue sites online and setting up appointments to see them." Eric tossed him a water bottle. "So if you've got a crisis, you're going to have to handle it."

"Not a crisis." Not yet. But shit, if the Summers brothers knew where their sister wanted to take their dinner last night—one wild night of no-holds-barred sex—Liam had a feeling this deal would blow up in his face. Or maybe they'd caught wind and the counteroffer was a form of payback? No, they'd come looking for him with their fists if they found out that Liam was trying to start something with their sister, not send a piece of paper.

"I have the counter from Brody," Liam said. "They're asking for a helluva lot more."

Eric sat at the edge of the desk. "What are the trucks worth?"

"About two hundred thousand apiece. They own ten in good working order. And their crew is top-notch. They also have agreements with some of our competitors to haul their timber. Smaller operations than yours, no major competitors on the list."

"Ours," Eric said.

Liam nodded. That word still felt tenuous, as if his claim to Moore Timber would dissolve if he didn't close this deal.

"They're worth something," Liam said, handing Eric the offer. "We'll need more information to find out how much. But I know it doesn't add up to this."

Eric frowned. "Brody gave every indication that they were facing hard times. But this number says otherwise."

Liam ground his teeth together, glancing around at the office walls. A few weeks ago, he'd sat here and agreed to take an equity stake in Moore Timber in exchange for helping out on the business side of things. But now he couldn't escape the feeling that failure was nipping at his heels. Give him a chainsaw and a tract of land that needed to be harvested and he'd tackle it in a heartbeat. Out in the forest, he knew which trees to cut when, how long they needed to be when they hit the landing, and how to manage his crew. Buying companies, reviewing financials—this was a different world.

But he hated the idea of walking away. His father had spent his entire life working in the forest. And in the end, he'd had nothing to show for it but a pile of medical bills from a swift-moving cancer. Liam wanted to prove he was worth more, that he deserved his empty office down the hall. He had to find a way to close this deal.

"We need to talk to the Summers brothers," Liam said.

"You're right." Eric handed him back the piece of paper. "Have Leah set something up for Monday. We have to finish the thinning over on that piece of BLM land this week and complete the clear-cut for Wilson's widow. I need you on those jobs while I find a place to marry your sister."

Liam nodded; the image of Brody, Chad, and Josh sitting around the conference table, staring him down, formed in his mind. And the night before, Liam had his hands all over their little sister. Again. If Liam had his way he would take it further.

But he had to close this deal first. He couldn't blow this chance to cement his future.

He couldn't allow his friendship with his business partner to disintegrate either. And it might, if Liam didn't come clean. Reaching for the door, he turned to Eric. "I took Katie out last night. We planned to talk about the deal. She was feeling left out of the conversation. But it turned into more."

His best friend frowned. "Do her brothers know?"

"No. And I don't plan to tell them. I'll leave that up to Katie." He didn't have to tell his friend why. Eric knew how things ended last time.

"Brody, Chad, and Josh might find out anyway. You may want to hold off on seeing her again until after we close this deal."

Liam shook his head. "I can't. Not if she plans to take that job in Montana."

"You're trying to give her a reason to stay?"

"I can't let her go again. The timing stinks. I know that, trust me. But I can't stay away any longer. Katie, she is . . ." Liam ran his hand through his hair. There was only one word running through his mind. *Mine*.

Eric crossed over, slapping him on the shoulder. "I get it, man. Believe me, I do. But do us both a favor and find a way to tell Katie before we sit down with her brothers."

Chapter 7

"FEEL LIKE SADDLING your horses?"

Katie turned away from the mare she had cross-tied in the barn's center aisle, and found Liam leaning against the open door. He'd traded his work clothes for clean jeans, cowboy boots, and a button-down flannel shirt, sleeves rolled up to reveal his powerful forearms. "Shouldn't you be playing in the forest?"

"I started early. Spent the morning playing and the past few hours at my desk."

"Brody dropped off our response to your bid today." Katie turned back to the horse, running the brush down her neck. "I figured that would keep you tied up for a while."

"Eric and I plan to sit down with your brothers, and you if you're interested, on Monday morning. But I'm not here to talk about your family business." Liam stepped inside, moving slowly, and offered his hand to the skittish horse. "I have carrots in my pocket. Can I give him one?"

"Her. The mare's name is Princess." She gave the horse, a rescue that had abuse in her recent past, a reassuring pat. "And yes. She'd like a carrot."

Liam reached behind him and withdrew the treat from his back pocket. Breaking it in half, he offered the first piece to Princess.

"Do you always carry horse treats?"

His gaze locked on hers as the mare ate the second piece. "Only when I'm coming to visit you. So how about a ride?"

She shook her head. "I can't. I have plans tonight."

"Hot date?"

She heard the edge in his voice. It left her wondering what would happen if she said yes. Would he demand that she cancel? All because of one kiss on his bike? That long-held anger rose to the surface. Liam didn't have the right to make choices for her. He never had.

She drew her shoulders back, reaffirming her desire to seduce the man gently feeding her mare carrots. But with the meeting scheduled for Monday, and Liam's determination to take things slow, she didn't have much time.

"More like a research project." She hooked a lead line to Princess's halter and released the crossties. "I hadn't planned on taking a date with me. But you're welcome to ride along."

Liam trailed behind her as she led the horse into her stall and closed the door. "I'm game. What are we researching?"

"Surprise. I'll pick you up at eight. This time, I'm driving." She turned, leaning back against the stall door. "Plan on a late night."

He took a step back. "Katie—"

"And wear your dancing shoes."

WITH THE FULL moon rising in the Oregon night sky, Liam climbed into the passenger side of Katie's station wagon and reached for his seat belt.

"Want me to drive?" He'd never liked riding shotgun.

"You don't know where we're going."

"You could navigate." Seat belt secure, he looked over at her. She'd changed out of her usual jeans and T-shirt into a short, pale pink dress that did amazing things for her long legs. Hell, maybe she should drive. He'd rather watch her skirt inch higher on her legs.

She put the car in reverse and backed out of his driveway. "I can do both. Settle in. Relax. We're going to be here for a while."

"I like how you dress for research, but I'm wondering if my jeans and boots will make the cut." He glanced up at her profile. She'd blown out her hair again and put on makeup. A light coat of shiny gloss on her lips, which left her looking like she wanted to be kissed, and a dusting of something that highlighted her green eyes. "Mind telling me where we're headed?"

"Surprise. But I think you'll fit in just fine."

He shook his head. "You have an independent streak a mile wide, don't you?"

"I couldn't stay eighteen forever."

"Honey, you knew your own mind back then. Your headstrong spirit is part of the reason I never realized how innocent you were. I never imagined it was your first time."

She stole a quick glance at him before returning her attention to the road. Putting on her blinker, she steered the wagon onto the highway. "We don't need to talk about this."

"I think we do."

He hadn't been looking forward to this conversation, but he knew it needed to happen. She'd told him the other night that she didn't hold a grudge, but he suspected that was a lie. Maybe she hadn't admitted it to herself. Either way, if he wanted to move forward with Katie, they needed to revisit the past. Here, in her moving car, where he couldn't invite her to sit on his lap, was probably the best place.

And there was one question he'd been dying to ask for seven long years. One he should have addressed to her that night instead of shutting her out. "Why didn't you tell me it was your first time?"

"I was afraid you'd stop. I didn't want you to walk away."

"I would have," he cut in.

"I know. And I told myself that it didn't matter. I thought you—" She bit her lower lip as if trying to stop herself from letting another word escape.

"That I'd fallen in love with you?" He kept his voice soft and gentle as if speaking to one of her skittish horses. "Katie, I never meant to hurt you. Never. But I was young too. And pretty damn stupid. I wasn't looking for love back then."

"And now?" she demanded. "What are you looking for now?"

Liam hesitated, staring out the window. It was too soon to tell her that he wanted a second chance at that moment when she'd offered him her heart, her future, her everything. He needed more time to prove that he deserved her, show her that he'd cherish her. This time it would be about what she wanted and needed from him.

"I'm not as stupid as I was back then. I like to think I've learned from my mistakes."

"And yet here you are. Taking me out for a second time this week," she said, not bothering to mask her sarcasm. "What would my brothers think?"

"I'm planning to leave them out of it this time." At least until he'd won her, which sure as hell better happen by Monday.

"And if that's not possible?" she challenged.

"Like you said, you're not eighteen anymore. I would expect them to respect your decisions."

She let out a mirthless laugh and headed for the exit ramp. The sign overhead indicated they were approaching one of the nearby college towns.

"Am I allowed to know where we're going yet?" he asked.

"Big Buck's Country Bar. According to the reviews I read online, they have a mechanical bull."

His gaze fixed on the bare skin of her thighs. "And you're planning to ride it wearing that?"

"No."

Thank God. He'd have ended up in a bar fight if she'd mounted the machine in that dress.

"We're just checking the place out. I want to find out if they have dancing. See if it gets too crowded. And if I can, talk to a manager, ask if they allow dogs."

Dancing and dogs? Liam furrowed his brow, unable to piece this puzzle together. "You lost me."

"It's for Georgia. The guest list for her party includes a friend with a service dog. I get the sense he's not a purse dog we could keep hidden. And Georgia wants to go dancing."

Katie turned into a parking lot lined with cars and a few motorcycles. The neon sign in the corner read: "Big Buck's, Live Music Tonight!" She pulled into a vacant space. "This doesn't look promising. I don't want your sister to run away and hide at her own party, not when we're supposed to be celebrating her last hurrah as a single woman."

Liam reached for her arm, stopping her from exiting the wagon. "Hold up a minute. We're here 'researching' my little sister's bachelorette party?"

She nodded. The smile on her face—it was almost devilish.

"Not a chance, Katie."

Her eyes sparkled with a naughty glint. "I can go in by myself."

His mind filled with the image of Katie's long legs wrapped around a mechanical bull. Every man in there would be staring at her. And when she got off and hit the dance floor? They'd be lining up for a chance to get close to her.

"Hell no." He let go of her arm and reached for the car door. "I'm coming with you."

KATIE SLAMMED HER door and turned around. Closing her eyes, she drew a deep breath, needing a moment before she played the part of the determined seductress again. She'd been having fun with her role. But then Liam had mentioned the L-word—the one that had no place in her plan.

That one word had thrown her off course. She'd started asking the wrong questions. Instead of wondering if he was ready to fall in love, she should be pressing to find out why he was demanding a place in her life now, after all this time.

She knew from experience that Liam always took charge, claiming what he wanted. That was part of who he was. He issued commands. But while his words haunted her fantasies, she knew they'd wreak havoc on her dreams for the future.

Still, when he spoke of respecting her choices, her heart had surged as if it wanted to send hope rushing through her veins. It was as if the stupid organ wanted to hear him out, find out if things would be different this time. Not that words and promises could change the past.

And if she wanted to keep her grandfather's company from slipping away, she had to follow her plan. She couldn't let her family down again. Her brothers accepted her choices, most of the time. But they had a limit. And when they found out she was involved with Liam again? She had a feeling that respect would go out the window in a heartbeat.

She'd seen the looks her brothers had given Liam over the past seven years. Back when Georgia had come to stay with her, before her friend had worked out her problems with the man she planned to marry, Katie's brothers—especially Chad—had been ready and willing to start a fight when Liam had come looking for his little sister.

Liam came around to her side of the car. "Ready?"

She walked past him. "Let's check it out."

She stepped inside Big Buck's, her eyes wide. This place looked nothing like the bar described on the review Web sites. The long wooden bar running along one side of the open space fit the pictures, but the similarities stopped there.

"Looks like they removed the mechanical bull," Liam said, standing close, his front practically touching her back. But glancing around, he didn't have much choice. Big Buck's was packed. People, mostly students from the nearby university, if she had to guess, covered every inch of space, their bodies moving to the bump-and-grind music.

"They do have dancing," he added, his lips brushing against her ear, sending a shiver down her spine. "But call me crazy, that doesn't sound like country."

"It's not." The floor beneath her sandals vibrated as the speakers pumped out the kind of music that called for close-contact movement.

"Do you still want to find a manager and ask if they allow dogs?" His hand wrapped around her middle, drawing her back as a pair of drunken girls wobbled past on their outrageously high heels.

"This place is all wrong for Georgia's bachelorette," she said, turning her head and looking up at him in order to be heard as she mentally crossed "Country-Western bar with a mechanical bull" off the list.

"Should we head out?" he asked.

His powerful, imposing body acted like a cocoon, shielding her from the wild scene in the bar. The way he held her—possessive and protective—she should run for the door.

"Katie?" he said. "It's your call."

She rested her head against his shoulder, silently debating. Stay or go? His arm, wrapped around her center, held her tight. Her hands moved to his forearm, feeling the corded muscles.

"We came all this way," she said. "Let's stay for a drink."

Liam released his hold, laced his fingers through hers, and stepped in front of her. Blazing a path to the bar, he kept her close behind him. Despite the press of bodies, she could smell his unique scent—a lingering hint of the forest mingled with a spicy men's cologne that drew her in and made her want to stay pressed against him.

Being here, in this bar, she felt as if she'd taken a step back in time. She'd visited places like this, dancing all night, while in college. At first, she'd been trying to erase the hurt she'd left back home, and later she'd come just for fun. Glancing over her shoulder at the crowd of people, couples mixed with groups of mostly girls dancing as if they didn't have a care in the world, Katie wished she could lose herself in that carefree feeling just for a little while.

"What do you want?" Liam kept his hold on her as he signaled the bartender.

"Something fruity and fun."

He raised an eyebrow.

The bartender came over before she could reply. Liam relayed her instructions to the young man and ordered a glass of water for himself.

"We don't do fancy drinks here, man," the bartender said. "Will vodka and cranberry work?"

She glanced over her shoulder at the crowded dance floor. The rhythm made her want to move, to feel Liam pressing close, dancing with her. Katie turned to the bartender. "Can I change my order to a shot of tequila?"

The bartender cracked a smile. "Sure thing."

He returned a minute later with their drinks. Katie downed hers and turned to the dance floor. "Drink up. We need to get out there."

Liam set his water back on the bar and took her hand, leading her around the side of the dance floor. On the edge of the crowd in a dimly lit corner, he drew her close.

His hands on her hips, he allowed her to set the rhythm. The shot combined with the frantic, building beat of the unfamiliar music and left her feeling bold. This man, this solid wall of enticing muscle—he'd made his desire clear the other night in the restaurant. And out here, in this wild crush of people, she wanted to lead him past words, drawing him headlong into touching, feeling.

She ran her hands down his chest, over his chiseled abs, and around to his back. Drifting lower still, she pressed her palms against his butt. He allowed her to pull him close.

"Katie," he growled.

"No words this time," she said. "Show me."

"Here?"

She nodded.

Without warning, he spun her around and drew her back flush against his chest. His arms banded around her, his palms pressed flat against her stomach. He guided her back, away from the dance floor and into the shadows. As they moved closer to the large subwoofer resting on the floor, shaking the ground beneath their feet, it was impossible to hear anything but the music. If he wanted to issue commands, he would need to use his hands and body.

Katie let out a low moan. This was her seduction. But the way his hands moved, brushing her thigh, running up the bare flesh, dipping below the hem of her skirt— he'd taken over.

His touch—it was wild and wicked. She'd craved this for so long, the way he never held back. She knew desire. But Liam ignited her needs in a way no other man ever had.

His hand moved higher, slipping beneath the fabric of her dress. Drawing soft, teasing circles on her inner thigh, sweeping closer and closer, then pulling away. She shifted, trying to guide his hand to her center. There were people all around, but she no longer cared. She needed this, him—now.

"Patience, honey." His lips brushed her ear. "I'll get you there."

His voice blended with the music, barely audible, but still she clung to the promise. His fingers circled higher, brushing the fabric of her underwear. She widened her stance, offering him access. But he didn't take it. His fingers remained outside the barrier, gliding back and forth. Teasing her, playing with the pressure, he drew her closer and closer.

She reached behind her, grabbing hold of his thighs, wanting to touch him. Again, she waited for his hands to slip beneath her underwear, but instead he brushed the pad of his thumb over the one place that needed him most.

"Liam," she gasped. "Oh God, Liam."

The music was too loud. He couldn't hear her. But she couldn't stop saying his name, hoping he'd deliver more. She rocked her hips, arching her back, asking with her body for what she wanted.

Without releasing her, he drew her further into the dark corner. Not that anyone was paying them any attention. They were too busy dancing, grinding against each other.

"They can't see," Liam said, his lips still touching her ear. "They don't know. This is just for you. For us."

Hearing those words, Katie froze. No one knew for now. But she planned to change that. And if her brothers caught them now . . .

No. She wished to keep this moment for herself. Next time, she'd stick to her plan. Tonight, in this not-so-country bar, she wanted to experience the man who'd once captured her heart. In this place where they couldn't go too far, she wanted Liam.

Rocking her hips against the bulge in his jeans, she silently asked for more. His fingers answered her plea, teasing her, drawing her closer and closer . . .

But she didn't want to be the only one lost in need. Gliding her hand up, she pressed her palm against the hard ridge of his erection.

"Lower your arm." He punctuated his command with a nip at her ear. "This is for you."

Ignoring him, she moved her hand up and down against his jeans, wishing she could slip her fingers beneath. But the darkness, the music, it only offered the illusion of privacy.

His teeth grazed her ear a second time while his thumb pressed lightly against the one place guaranteed to skyrocket her into orgasm territory. "You're not listening?"

"No." She ran her palm down his length, cupping him through his jeans.

"Katie." Hearing the warning mixed with desire in his tone, she didn't let go, refusing to obey. This time.

Liam thrust against her hand and a thrill coursed through her. She wanted him out of his mind with lust—right back where they'd started seven years ago.

Only this time, she'd keep her L-words straight.

Chapter 8

BENEATH THE LUST blanketing his common sense, Liam knew that this was too much, too fast. They needed more time to get to know each other again, and to move on from the past. But when he was with Katie, the pull was so damn strong.

And the way she refused to move her hand, to stop torturing him here, in a dark corner where he couldn't do a damn thing about it . . . Liam closed his eyes and groaned. Thank God for his jeans. Without the barrier, he wouldn't be able to hold back. Not after all this time. Not with her.

Releasing her hip, he ran his hand over her ass, over the fabric of her dress as the song ended and another one started. He paused, giving her one light, playful squeeze before lifting his hand away an inch.

"Planning to punish me?" she said, her voice heavy with need as his other hand continued to tease her.

He was tempted, but he wrapped his fingers around her hip, holding tight. "Not here. Not yet."

But the thought of it turned him on. Drawing her underwear aside, his fingers slipped beneath, searching for her entrance. Touching her—it wasn't enough. But for tonight, it had to be.

Katie turned her head to the side and he watched her lips form his name. The music had grown too loud again. He couldn't hear. But he knew. Here, in the dark corner of a college bar, she wanted him. All other thoughts vanished, leaving him with only one—*Don't let go.*

Liam scanned the crowd to ensure no one was glancing at their dark corner of the room. His thumb brushed her sweet spot. The one place he knew would drive her wild. As much as he wanted to draw this out, he couldn't. They didn't have the luxury of time.

His lips touched her ear. "Come for me. Now."

He felt her body tense. The hand rubbing the front of his jeans stilled. It was as if she'd been waiting for those words.

And then she exploded. Liam watched as her eyes closed and her lips parted. Maybe it was the way she moved her lips, or her silent cry, but he swore he saw the same sense of awe and wonder in her expression that he'd witnessed years ago. That look—it pushed past the physical, touching something deep inside him.

Katie stepped forward, breaking free from his hold as she adjusted her skirt.

He smiled down at her, tucking a strand of hair behind her ear. "Want another drink, or are you ready to go?"

She stared out at the crowd for a moment before turning to him. Moving closer, she ran her hand up his thigh, stopping short of his crotch. "I think I've done enough research for one night. And you might be more comfortable in the car."

Her words held a sensual promise. Before he could tell her that he planned to take a rain check, she abandoned their quiet corner, weaving her way through the crowd toward the door. Liam followed close behind. Outside, in the cool night air, they headed for her wagon.

"I'll need your keys," he said, holding out his hand.

Katie turned, leaning back against the trunk. "In a hurry to get home? Without even a good-night kiss?"

She took his hand, pulling him close. Staring down into her green eyes, Liam placed one hand on either side of her head, palms flat against the wagon. Moving closer until his thigh touched hers, he leaned down and brushed her lips, a simple, chaste kiss.

"I'm done with stolen moments in parking lots, or out under trees," he said. "Next time, I want a bed."

Her hands reached for his hips, trying to draw him closer. He didn't budge. This was too important. If he wanted to find his way back to the moment when she'd looked at him, her eyes filled with love, he couldn't rush to the finish line.

"What makes you think there will be a next time?" she said, her tone light and teasing.

"I'm not giving up on you. On us. Not this time."

KATIE STARED INTO his brown eyes. She still felt the lingering effect of his touch. When this man took over, her body obeyed as if acting on pure instinct. She'd made plans, dammit. But he touched her and she set them aside.

Turning her gaze to the full moon high in the sky above them, she struggled to collect her thoughts, one question rushing to the forefront. She looked back to him, taking in the hard line of his jaw, set and determined.

"Why now?" she asked. "Is it because of my family's company?"

His gaze sharpened. "Hell no. If anything, I should steer clear of you until the deal is done."

"Then why?"

"Because I didn't have anything to offer you back then." He stepped back, lifted his hands, running them through his short hair.

"That morning, in the field, I saw the love and hope in your eyes, and I panicked," he continued. "I was one year out of school, living at home and caring for my mom while she battled cancer, knowing she was losing the fight. I was following in my father's footsteps, working in the industry that had kept a roof over our heads and food on the table, but not much more."

"I wasn't asking you for anything," she said. She had stupidly believed she'd already won his heart.

"Honey, you looked at me like I was your future, and I was taking life one day at a time. I wasn't ready. And shit, I'm sorry I led you on. I'm sorry for the way it ended."

He was sorry. Hearing that now snuffed out her lingering desire, making room for the feelings she'd carried around for years.

"Most guys panic and they stop calling." Her voice trembled with the ancient hurt. "My brothers confronted you and you told them everything. You—"

"Not everything, Katie," he said.

"Liam, you said that you regretted what we'd done. You opened my eyes to a world of pleasure, and then you walked away, leaving me feeling as if I'd done something wrong."

Liam closed his eyes, bowing his chin to his chest. "At the time, I thought I was doing the right thing. Your brothers demanded that I leave you alone if I wasn't serious. And I refused to make promises that I knew would end up broken."

"Do you have any idea how embarrassed I was?" she said, pressing her palms flat against the side of the wagon as if the car could anchor her. "Look at me, Liam."

For once, he obeyed her.

"You could have told them it was none of their business," she continued. "Or you could have talked to me."

"I didn't know what to say to you, Katie. I met you out there because I couldn't stand to go home. I know it sounds awful, but I wasn't looking for love. I just needed a break." He shook his head, his hands falling to his sides. "Watching my parents struggle, knowing I was headed down the same road . . . I felt like my future was doomed. I didn't want to think about it."

"We both went to that field looking for an escape." She

felt the heat of her argument fade away. She understood loss. No, she couldn't imagine watching a parent die from a slow illness. But she knew the empty feeling of losing someone you loved. Forever.

"In the span of a few days, I lost my grandfather and my dad," she continued. "It was so sudden, so over-whelming. It took me a long time to recover."

"I know, honey. And I knew you were still grieving. It didn't stop me from meeting you under those trees. But it should have."

"No," she said, her voice firm. "I didn't need you to make that choice for me. I wanted to be with you. Every-thing else in my life felt as if it was beyond my control. It felt as if my life was happening to me."

"Katie." He reached for her. She held up her hand, unwilling and unable to let him touch her. She had so much she needed to tell him, and suddenly it felt as if she couldn't wait.

"That's what hurt the most. You made the decision that I was too young to handle breaking up with you. All by yourself."

"I won't make that mistake again," he said, meeting her gaze. "I swear."

No, he wouldn't. He'd never get the chance. This time she was calling the shots. And she'd never let him get close enough to hurt her again. But still, hearing those words, part of her wished she could believe him.

Or maybe it was the lingering effects of his wild touch. An orgasm like that—it messed with a girl's mind.

The ring of her phone cut through her thoughts. Turning her attention away from Liam and orgasms, she pulled out her cell and glanced at the screen.

"Hi Chad," she answered, knowing her brother wouldn't call unless it was important. And he'd keep calling until he reached her.

"Katie," her brother said. "Where the hell are you?"

"Big Buck's," she said. "I'm checking out the bar for Georgia."

She thought about telling her brother that Liam was with her, but something in Chad's voice stopped her.

"You need to get back here right now," Chad said.

Her grip tightened on the phone. "Is something wrong? I'm about an hour away from home."

"The sheriff drove up about five minutes ago with a pair of rescued horses," Chad said. "I caught a glance inside, sis. They're skin and bones. The only sanctuary in the area is full right now. He wanted to know if we could take them for a while."

"Yes," she said, pulling the car key from her purse and handing it to Liam. Looking up at him, her lips formed one word. *Drive.*

"Brody is out there now," Chad continued. "And it doesn't look like he's unloading the trailer."

"Go back out there and tell the sheriff we'll take them." Katie opened the passenger side door. "We have space in the barn."

"Katie, I'm with you," Chad said. "But Brody doesn't want another mouth to feed."

"It's not his call," she said. "Tell Brody I'll pay for it."

She ended the call and secured her seat belt. In the pit of her stomach she had a bad feeling her big brother would ignore her. Brody had led the family for so long it was as if he'd forgotten that his siblings were adults now—especially her. And her big brother didn't have the right to make decisions for her.

"Katie?" Liam asked, turning the key to her wagon. "Are you OK?"

"Just drive." *For once, please listen to me. Let me call the shots and do as I ask.* "Please. I need to get home."

Chapter 9

LIAM STOLE A glance at his passenger. Her eyes were fixed on the road, her hands clutching her phone. He'd overheard enough of the call to get a sense of the situation.

"Can you go any faster?" she asked.

"Not if you want to get home in one piece," he said. "Have a little faith in your brother. I'm sure he'll do the right thing."

"Brody always thinks he's right. But if he sends those poor animals away, with no place else to go . . ." She shook her head. "How much longer?"

"Honey, we've only been in the car for five minutes." It would take them another forty-five to get back to Independence Falls. "Sit back and try to relax."

She grunted as if he'd suggested the impossible.

"Tell me, do you have any other places in mind for Georgia's party?" Liam asked, hoping the conversation would distract Katie from her burning desire to get home.

"I do," she said. "But the research for the next idea on the list, well, let's just say it is a little more involved."

"Than a mechanical bull?"

She nodded. "I want to check out a place on the west side of the Independence Falls Reservoir. I was hoping to drive over Saturday."

"That side of the lake is surrounded by national forest. You'll need to park your car a ways out and hike in."

"I know, but it's the next thing on Georgia's list. And after seeing the bar tonight, probably the most practical."

"As her brother, I vote for hiking and camping. But getting to that side of the reservoir is a mile and half mostly uphill." Liam had no doubt Georgia could do it. She had traveled on foot while hauling a seriously heavy pack when stationed in Afghanistan. But the others?

"That's one helluva way to kick off a bachelorette party," he added.

"I know," Katie said. "And getting everything out there will be a challenge."

Liam stole another glance at her. She'd relaxed her death grip on her phone. "Everything? What are you planning to bring to the party?"

"Trust me, you don't want to know. It's one of your sister's wild ideas, but Eric would hate it. And if we have to hike out there, it won't happen anyway."

"You could come at it from the other side. Cross the water by boat," Liam said, knowing he should stay out of it. If Eric would hate Georgia's plans, he probably would too. But the thought of more "research" with Katie kept the wheels in his mind turning.

"I have a friend who owns a small motorboat and docks it over there. We might be able to borrow it," he continued. "If the water level isn't too low this time of year."

She cocked her head to one side as if considering the idea. "Too low even for a motorboat?"

"The reservoir is manmade on cleared land. Lots of stumps underneath when the water level is low. And we've had a dry few months."

They were nearing the end of fire season, but this one had been rough. A few weeks earlier, Liam had fought a massive blaze on a piece of property he'd been harvesting. And afterward, he'd faced an investigation that had nearly cost him his job and his best friend. He was more than ready for the constant rains the Pacific Northwest was known for, but Mother Nature wasn't cooperating.

"But I'll make the call," Liam added. "Are you free this weekend?"

"Saturday might work. I would need to see about the cabin first. And make some other arrangements."

"Saturday's great. If you don't mind heading out in the late afternoon. We're planning to get the last of the trees on Mrs. Wilson's property harvested that morning." And thank goodness for that. He wanted the excuse to stay the night with her alone in a cabin. After tonight, in the club, feeling her respond to his touch, he wanted her. But he planned to take his time. He'd meant what he'd said in the parking lot. He needed to do this right.

THIRTY MINUTES LATER, Katie dropped Liam off on the street in front of his house with a promise to call the cabin about Saturday, and sped toward home. Turning down the driveway, her hands tightened around the steering as the house came into view. There was no sign of the horse trailer. But her big brother sat on the front porch.

Katie parked her wagon and climbed out, fighting to control her temper. She approached Brody, noting the way his eyes widened at the sight of her dress.

"Where are the horses?" she demanded.

"They're in the barn." He pushed off the steps, shoving his hands in his pockets. "Chad and Josh are feeding them now."

Temper gave way to a flood of relief. Katie rushed over and threw her arms around her big brother, her face resting against his T-shirt. "Thank you. The whole drive back, I was so scared you would send them away."

"The sheriff was out of options. We were his last hope. And I would hate to see them go to a slaughterhouse." Brody hugged her back, but then drew away, looking down at her. "But we can't afford to keep them, Katie."

"We'll have the money soon," she said. "When the contract comes through and we put those new trucks to use—"

"I should never have let you buy those trucks." Brody released her, stepping back. "We're out a lot of money if Black Hills doesn't sign. And I think Eric and Liam can smell our desperation."

"Mr. Fidderman will come through," she insisted.

And she wasn't desperate. But she had a bad feeling her brothers—Brody in particular—saw Moore Timber's offer as their only option.

"Brody, do you want to sell to Moore Timber?"

Her brother ran his hand over his face. "I think it might be best. At some point, we need to take what we can get for the business and move on with our lives. You have a potential job waiting for you in Montana. Josh wants—"

"Stop," she demanded. "You've put us first for the past seven years. You held us together after Dad died. It was always about us. Now it is time to think about what you want."

"I'm proud of what we've built here," Brody said quietly. "But—"

"No more 'buts.'" Katie crossed her arms in front of her chest. "We're not selling."

Brody shook his head. "You're just like them. Dad and Grandpa. So damn stubborn."

Katie smiled, feeling a rush of pride at his words. Those men were her heroes. And though her brother might not realize it, she had fought an uphill battle to keep her backbone, to make her own choices. "Have a little faith in me, Brody. I can close the deal with Black Hills. Once we have those contracts, we can start to grow the business. Eventually, Chad, Josh, and I can step away."

"What about Montana?"

"If I get the papers signed, and *if* they offer me the job, maybe I'll take it. If not, well, I'm a big girl Brody, I'll find something else eventually." Katie looped her arm through his. "How about you introduce me to the new horses?"

"Do you want to change first?" Brody asked, looking pointedly at her skirt.

"Horses first."

Arm in arm, they headed for the barn. "Mind telling me where you were dressed like that?"

"I was checking out a potential bar for Georgia's bachelorette party."

The muscles in her brother's jaw tightened. "You went barhopping by yourself?"

"No. I brought a friend," she said. "Don't worry, he kept me safe."

From the other guys, she thought. But if Liam thought for one minute that a heartfelt conversation in a parking lot would erase the old hurt she'd carried around for the past seven years, he was flat-out wrong. She wasn't about to hand back the apology, but knowing why he'd walked out of her life after one heart-to-heart with her brothers didn't change the fact that her loyalties lay elsewhere.

"Thanks again, Brody." She gave his arm a squeeze. "For everything."

Chapter 10

"WE'RE NOT SELLING the company to Moore Timber," Katie assured the balding man with the weathered face. Joe Fidderman, owner of Black Hills Timber, nodded. But his hand holding the pen over the signature line of the contracts did not move.

"I have nothing against Eric. I knew his father well and he's grown up to be a fine young man. The way he has grown that business . . ." Mr. Fidderman shook his head. "We're not competing in the same league anymore."

"You're branching out into different areas." Katie forced a smile as she tried not to stare at the hand holding the pen above the paper. "By letting us take away the branches and other typically unused pieces from your timber harvests, you're helping to create energy. All of that material will be turned into biomass fuel. And at the same time, we're cleaning up the forest floor. Some would argue that alone will help prevent forest fires."

Mr. Fidderman nodded, lowering the pen to the paper.

"Eric Moore is not interested in biomass," she added. "We are."

"If you're sure your brothers don't want to sell—"

"Sir, I won't lie to you," she said. "Part of me wants to sell and move on with my life. But my oldest brother loves the company. Brody has worked so hard to keep it running. When my dad died . . . Brody was there for us. He found a way to pay for my college tuition even though times were tight. He could have moved away, pursued his own passions, but instead he set everything aside for us. For me. And he's not ready to sell."

Mr. Fidderman nodded. "Well then, you have yourself a deal, Ms. Summers."

Katie held her breath as the older man scrawled his signature across the contract. She'd done it. She'd secured the future of Summers Family Trucking. She stood, reaching across the desk to take the papers.

"I look forward to working with you," he said.

Katie tightened her grip on the contracts. "And my brothers."

"But you're the one with the vision. I like that about you," he said, finally releasing the documents she'd been dying to get her hands on. "I feel confident that with you steering this ship, we stand to make a pretty penny."

Forcing a smile, she nodded. Montana was sounding more and more impossible. Of course, they had not offered her the job. Yet. She'd aced the interview this morning. But still, if Brody had walked away from them when opportunity came his way after their dad died, she never would have finished college.

"Of course. And in time, I think you'll find you like working with Brody. He knows this business inside and out."

"I understand loyalty," Mr. Fidderman said. "I respect what you're doing for them. Keeping the company afloat. It's not an easy thing to do in this market. I think we'll make good partners. And if this helps prevent forest fires, I'm all for it. Lord knows I can't afford another one on my land. The last one, about two years back, nearly wiped me out."

Katie said good-bye and walked out of the Black Hills office clutching the contracts to her chest. She'd done it. Now they didn't need Moore Timber or Liam Trulane. Of course she still needed to convince Chad and Josh that walking away from a million dollars—or more if Liam raised the offer—made sense.

In her back pocket, her cell phone vibrated. Setting the contracts on the hood of the car, she retrieved it and glanced at the screen. Montana. And there was only one person there who had a reason to call her—Carol Lewis, owner of the Safe Haven.

"Hello?" she answered, biting back the words: *Did I get the job?*

"Katie, this is Carol Lewis. I spoke with your sheriff. He told me about the horses you rescued last night."

"Actually, my brother was home and accepted them," she said.

"Because you insisted. Katie, I'm impressed with your

knowledge of finance. But that's not why I'm offering you the position. I want to leave the Safe Haven with someone who will always put the animals first. The business side is important. And heaven knows, I couldn't run this place without donations. But at the end of the day, it is about loving the animals no one else wants."

"It is," Katie said, staring out at the mountains. On the other side of those peaks stood her family's barn filled with misfit horses and goats. Animals who depended on her, who needed—

"Wait, did you just offer me the job?" Katie said.

Carol Lewis laughed. "Yes. I did. So what do you say?"

Yes. The word was on the tip of her tongue. "Thank you," Katie said, closing her eyes. "I'm thrilled and honored. But I . . . I need a few days to think about it."

"Of course. It is a big move and I don't wish to rush you. However, I'm leaving soon and need to make sure the Safe Haven is in good hands."

"I understand. I'll have an answer for you soon. I promise." Katie ended the call and set her phone down on the hood of her wagon beside the contracts.

"I got the job," she whispered, staring out at the familiar scenery. But the triumph was bittersweet. Brody and her brothers needed her here. Part of her wanted to say yes, but she had a feeling that wasn't the right thing to do for her family.

LIAM LEANED AGAINST his car, his phone in his hand. He texted Katie, telling her they were set for tomorrow's trip to the cabin. He'd managed to push the fact that this was a "research" trip for his little sister's bachelorette to the far corners of his mind. He was going for Katie. An entire night alone with her . . .

A response flashed on his screen. *I'll meet you at the reservoir dock. And I have a few surprises for you.*

Grinning like a fool, Liam pushed off his car and headed for the front door to Moore Timber and down the hall. Surprises? As long as they didn't interfere with his plans to earn her trust, to show Katie that he needed and wanted her in his life, he was game to experiment. They had been pretty creative under the twin fir trees seven years ago, but he'd learned a lot since then. He had a few ideas of ways to make her scream his name again and again.

"Whatever you're thinking, I'm guessing it has little to nothing to do with Wilson's widow's land," Eric mused, his shoulder resting against the doorway to his office.

Liam chuckled. "Nope. But we're done over there. Josh Summers hauled the last load from the landing a few hours ago."

"Good. Come in and have a drink. I need to fill you in on my chat with my friend Tim Granger. Remember him? He's the number two at Black Hills Timber." Eric returned to his desk chair and started leafing through papers.

Liam followed him, collapsing into one of the leather chairs across from Eric's desk. "Yeah, I know Tim. Good guy."

Eric walked to the mini-fridge and pulled out two waters, tossing one to Liam. "Turns out his boss just signed a contract with Summers Family Trucking to haul the excess from their harvests to the biomass plant."

"That's what the new trucks and the chipper are for," Liam said, leaning back in his chair.

"With that deal, they're worth more than we thought," Eric said. "But I couldn't figure out why they didn't tell us about the pending contract. And then Tim told me who negotiated the deal. It was all Katie."

Liam knew he should be pissed that she'd hidden this from him, but his pride in her swelled. "All by herself?"

"Maybe. I think her brothers know, but they still want to sell. I suspect Brody thinks the company is holding his siblings back, Katie in particular. And he'll want to do what is best for his family. He's always put their interests first."

"Then Katie's the driving force behind the counteroffer too."

"That's my guess." Eric placed his elbows on his desk. "After talking with Tim, I can tell you one thing. Any deal we negotiate with Summers Family Trucking should include her."

Every muscle in his body tensed. "You want her to work here? For Moore Timber?"

Eric nodded. "Her forward-thinking business sense makes Katie one of Summers Family Trucking's biggest assets."

"She's not going to like that. She plans to take that job in Montana if they offer it."

"Maybe not, but I get the feeling she'll understand. You're seeing her this weekend, right?"

"I am." Liam frowned. "But I wasn't planning to talk shop."

"I'm not asking you to discuss mergers and acquisitions over dinner. I don't want to tip our hand until Monday's meeting, which by the way needs to include her. But it would be great if she had another reason to stay in Independence Falls."

Liam lifted his bottle of water to his lips and quickly drained it. He needed to make the right decision for Moore Timber. His best friend since grade school had trusted him with a piece of the business. Liam damn well better do right by Eric.

But the thought of spending Saturday night with Katie and not telling her about Eric's offer—it felt wrong. And when it came to Katie, he'd already screwed up.

"There is a lot of money to be made in this area," Eric continued. "I don't have the connections. Hell, I spoke out against it at the state loggers' association years ago when it was first introduced. My father was against it and I followed his lead. Most of the leaders in this area probably wouldn't take my calls."

Liam lowered his empty bottle. "But they'd talk to Katie."

"They would. The industry has changed. And we need to move with it," Eric said. "I plan to hand Moore Timber over to Nate one day. And when I do, I want it to be a thriving company."

"I get it man, I do." Liam wanted to leave a piece of this business to his kids one day too, not just a pile of bills marked overdue like his dad had left behind. "But I can't hurt her again."

"I'm not asking you to trick her into selling, working here, or even staying," Eric said. "Just move up your time-table. Do whatever you need to do to make her see that she has a future here."

As if his friend's words had opened a window to his dreams, Liam pictured Katie living with him in the house he planned to build on the land. They'd keep her animals. All of them. His imagination ran wild, adding a barn to the property for her horses and riding trails cut through the woods.

He wanted to turn that fantasy into reality. But if she suspected he'd tried to manipulate her, even for a minute, she'd walk away and never look back.

Liam turned and headed for the door. "I'll see what I can do."

Chapter 11

Katie stared out at the smooth surface of the lake. The water level was low, but Liam's friend had agreed to let them take the boat. She'd reserved a "luxury" cabin on the other side, though she suspected that clean sheets and hot water were the owner's definition of lavish amenities.

And an outdoor shower. The boudoir photographer had pointed that out to her. Apparently Clive Jones from Stolen Moments Photography loved working with water.

She glanced over her shoulder at the empty parking area. Both Liam and Mr. Jones should be here any minute. She planned to take the boudoir photographer with them, let him check out the location, and determined if he was a creep. Then they would take him back. And she would seduce Liam at the cabin.

In her postage stamp of a hometown, it wouldn't take long for word to get back to her brothers that she'd spent the night with Liam. It had taken less than twenty-four hours seven years ago.

Of course, she could play cards with Liam all night and still probably spark her brothers' tempers. Once the rumors started, what really happened in the cabin wouldn't matter. But the thought of being alone with Liam and *not* touching him . . . impossible. Not with the memory of that orgasm in Big Buck's burned into her memory.

The sound of tires hitting the gravel parking area drew her attention. Spotting Liam's truck, she forced a smile and waved. He pulled into the space beside her wagon, opened the driver's side door, and hopped down.

"Hi, honey." The familiar endearment, the low timber of his voice that had been part of her life for so long— and her fantasies—pushed at her guilt. He'd apologized for the past. Offered explanations. They had both been young, stupid, and hurting.

Maybe she should abandon her plan. After all, she had the signed contract with Black Hills.

Katie frowned. She'd presented the contracts to her brothers after her meeting with Mr. Fidderman. But still, Brody had insisted that they sit down with Eric and Liam on Monday. Typical Brody, he didn't like the fact that the deal with Black Hills would tie her to Independence Falls and prevent her from taking the job in Montana. And Josh had taken his side.

She needed to give her brothers another reason to re-consider selling to Moore Timber. And that left her with Liam.

Studying the man in front of her, Katie drew her lower lip between her teeth. His T-shirt hugged his muscular back as he turned and reached into the bed of his truck. He withdrew a small duffel and returned for more. Her gaze drifted south, admiring the way his cargo shorts fit his butt.

Yes, she wanted to push her brothers away from the deal with Moore Timber. But maybe part of her simply wanted one more night with Liam Trulane.

"What's in the bags?" she asked.

"We needed supplies." Liam withdrew two shopping bags from the back of his truck. "I wanted to cook dinner for you tonight. But don't worry, there's no bacon in there."

"You didn't have to go shopping." She'd tossed a jar of sauce and a box of pasta in her bag, figuring that would be enough.

Liam set the groceries beside his duffel. Standing in front of her, so close she could run her hands over his chest and feel the muscles beneath his faded "Moore Timber" T-shirt, he smiled at her, his brown eyes warm and welcoming. "I told you before, I'm doing things right this time."

She shoved her hands in her pockets. Maybe no one would find out about tonight. Maybe her plan would fail. The thought of being with him, free from the complications of family and revenge—

"Katie Summers?"

Katie stepped to the side, moving away from Liam and the way his powerful presence toyed with her common sense and disrupted her plans. A tall young man, who looked like he belonged in front of the lens instead of behind it, smiled as he headed toward them, one camera around his neck and a bag in his hand.

The photographer set his bag down and offered his hand. "Clive Jones."

"Yes." She smiled, noting the firm way he shook her hand. His skin was smooth, so different from the rough, callused feel of Liam's touch. "Nice to meet you, Mr. Jones."

"Please call me Clive," he said, flashing a smile that screamed, *I was a male model in a past life.*

"And you are?" Liam demanded.

"The photographer from Stolen Moments Photography." He beamed at Liam before turning to the lake. "This place is stunning. The light on the water . . ." Clive raised his camera.

"Photographing nature is my first love," Clive continued over the snap, snap, snap of his high-end digital equipment. "Don't get me wrong, I'm passionate about Stolen Moments. Combine nature with beautiful women? It doesn't get much better. I can't wait to see the cabin. And that outdoor shower."

Clive gave her a wink. She'd spoken to him on the phone, but Katie had harbored the idea that a man who took pictures of women in seductive poses would be creepy, looking at her as if envisioning her naked. This man was playful and enthusiastic, but minus the slimy dude/serial killer vibe. Thank goodness.

"He's coming with us?" Liam turned to her, hands on his hips.

"To get a sense of the setting," Clive explained. "Katie wanted to meet in person and show me the location for the photo shoot in advance of the party."

"Photo shoot?" Liam said. "Katie, if this is one of your surprises—"

"Mr. Jones is a boudoir photographer." Out of the corner of her eyes, she saw Clive move away as if sensing they needed space to talk. Smart man. But given his line of work, he had to land in number of awkward situations.

"A what?" Liam demanded.

"He sets up intimate photo shoots for women to share with their partners," she said, doing her best to quote the Web site. Her takeaway had been: *This man takes pictures of women in their underwear or less.* She had nothing against the idea if it made Georgia happy. But she had some concerns too, which was why she'd called his list of references first. All the women she spoke with raved about him.

"I wanted to meet him first. Make sure he wasn't crazy. I didn't want to meet him alone and he expressed an interest in seeing the cabin. It made sense to bring him along. Do a test run."

"Have you lost your mind?" The muscles in Liam's jaw jumped, his voice rising to the point that anyone—including the photographer—could hear them.

"It was Georgia's idea."

Liam closed his eyes, shaking his head. "I should have locked her in the spare bedroom when I had the chance."

"She wants her party to be special. Memorable. But we don't have a lot of options. Your sister can't handle crowds and there is no way I'm jumping out of a plane." She stepped back and turned toward the dock. "Let's head out so we can do a few trail shots, check the place out, and get Mr. Jones back before dark."

Liam caught her arm. "You're not taking your clothes off in front of that man."

The way he said those words, as if she didn't have a choice, as if the decision was his to make—it should have sparked fury. She hadn't planned to strip down for the photographer. Not today. Not while Liam watched. Still, he had no right to tell her what to do.

"Maybe not all—"

"No."

A thrill ran down her spine. Despite their history and the fact that she'd struggled to change, to become a different woman from the foolish girl who'd met him in the field, she wanted to see his brown eyes burn with a look that said, *You're mine.*

"Liam," she said, feeling as if she was poking an angry bear. "You might like the ones under the shower."

He drew her closer, his eyes shining with a look of pure possession. "Katie, when you get wet that man will not be anywhere close to you."

LIAM RELEASED KATIE's arm and headed for the man with the damn camera. If the guy wasn't looking to take pictures of Katie and, shit, his little sister, he might have slapped him on the back and asked how the hell he started a business taking pictures of mostly naked women. When he heard Clive Jones say Katie's name, Liam had known he'd hate the surprise.

Boudoir photographer wasn't the first thing running through his head. He'd seen the other guy and wondered if she had something wild planned for tonight. He was all for kinky sex. But he drew the line at sharing Katie—even if the guy planned to stay on the other side of the lens.

He stopped beside the photographer. "Sorry for your trouble, but you need to leave."

Clive Jones lowered his camera. "I take it she didn't tell you first. Look, man, I'm sorry. But if the bride changes her mind, I can leave your girlfriend out of it."

"The bride is my sister," Liam said. This man wasn't getting near Georgia. He reached into his back pocket and withdrew his wallet. "What do we owe you for your trouble?"

"Nothing." Clive Jones held up his camera. "The shots of the lake in this light were worth the trip."

"I'm sorry," Katie added, moving to Liam's side. "For dragging you down here. But the bride's fiancé would probably have a similar reaction to my friend here."

Her friend? Liam kept his mouth shut. But after tonight, they were going to be a lot more than friends. He'd taken this as slow as he could, fighting the attraction. Now he needed Katie in his life.

"Most guys, when they have the pictures in their hands, don't care who took them," Clive said, as he turned and headed to his car.

"I would," Liam muttered. "And so would Eric."

Liam scooped up his duffel and groceries, then turned to Katie. "Ready?"

"That wasn't your call." She picked up her bag and followed him down the small dock.

Liam set the bags beside the small blue and white motorboat. It wasn't much, but it would get them across the lake.

"If your sister wants a boudoir photo shoot, she should have one. After all she sacrificed, Georgia deserves fun and happiness—"

"She does," he agreed. "But I have a feeling that explaining those pictures to Eric wouldn't be much fun. You'll have to think of something else for her party."

"I will. Still, you didn't need to send him away before I got a chance to talk to him and see his work. I wanted to tell Georgia that I honestly explored the options."

Leaning over the edge of the boat, Katie set her bag on the wraparound bench. Liam moved behind her, wrapping his arm around her waist, capturing her body against his as she stood. She'd worn jeans and a fitted sleeveless shirt. Her clothes hugged her curves, but left him longing for the short skirt she'd worn to the bar.

"She can set up her own photo shoot. I'm sure Eric knows how to work a camera." Liam's lips brushed her ear. "But tonight, in the cabin, that's for us. To finish what we started at Big Buck's."

If he had his way, it wouldn't end with one night in a cabin.

She leaned back against him, her hands brushing his thighs. "It might have been fun. Like foreplay."

His hands moved to her hips, slowing turning her to face him. Liam lifted his fingers to her cheek, gently brushing her smooth skin. His lips followed. Katie touched his chest, palms flat against his T-shirt. Damn, he wished he could pull the fabric over his head and feel her skin against his. But this wasn't the place.

He deepened the kiss, running his tongue along her lips until she let him in. Her body pressed closer, seeking his. Her hands moved to his ass, holding him tight and drawing him in until Liam could feel her chest against his. Slowly, he drew back, kissing the edge of her mouth, her cheek, her jaw.

Brushing her hair away from her eyes, he looked down at her. "Honey, I know a thing or two about foreplay."

He slid one hand over the soft curve of her waist. Breaking their full-body contact, he lifted his hand, keeping his palm flat, brushing it back and forth against her breast. He was tempted to draw her shirt and bra away, touch her bare flesh. But first, he needed to get them to the cabin.

She pulled back, turning to the boat, offering him a heated look. "And you might be surprised what I've learned."

The lower half of his body responded to her words, standing at attention, ready and waiting for a demonstration.

"Get in the boat, Katie," he said, his voice a low growl. "Let's see how fast we can get this ship to the other side of the lake."

Once she'd climbed in, Liam released the ropes and

turned on the engine. He stood behind the wheel, guiding the motorboat into the reservoir.

"The water level is lower than I thought," he said. He'd already counted four stumps below the surface. Turning the wheel to avoid another, he tried to focus on getting to the other side with the boat in one piece. But with Katie seated behind him, her words and the feel of her lips, her skin, and her breasts fresh in his mind, it was a freaking battle.

The quiet, apart from the sound of the motor, allowed his mind to wander. Instead of watching for tree stumps, he pictured Katie's shirt rising up, revealing her breasts. His hand tightened around the steering wheel.

"I'm surprised your friend let you take the boat out," she said.

"I didn't give him much choice," Liam admitted. He'd told Marvin that he'd cover the damages if the boat crashed, and clean up the trees on his property. Given that Marvin owned thirty acres of forest that hadn't been limbed in years, it was a helluva bargain.

"If only Georgia knew how committed you are to planning her bachelorette party," Katie murmured.

He glanced over his shoulder as they crossed through the center of the lake. Her green eyes sparkled with mischief.

"You didn't need to stay overnight to check this place out," he said.

"No, I didn't."

She ran her tongue over her lips as she reached up, drawing her long, straight hair into a ponytail. Her gaze never wavered from his. That look—it was wicked and so damn enticing his balls ached. He was tempted to cut the engine and anchor here, in the middle of the water. But making love for the first time in years in a small, run-down, and barely seaworthy craft wasn't much better than the backseat of a car.

"I wouldn't have booked an overnight if you hadn't offered to keep me company," she added.

Knowing she was here for him gave him hope that the hot and wild need he felt for her ran both ways.

The boat lurched, shifting to the right. Liam turned her attention to the water, holding tight to wheel. Behind him, Katie tried to hold on, but ended up sliding down the bench as the boat stopped. Liam waited for them to move forward, drift with the tide. But the vessel remained still, stuck at the awkward angle.

Liam peered over the edge and spotted the stump resting beneath the right side of the boat. "Shit. I guess the water level was too low."

And he'd been distracted, looking at Katie when he should have been keeping careful watch for stumps. Liam studied the shore. It wasn't far to the dock. And the water wasn't deep here.

"Looks like we're going to get wet," he said.

"We're swimming to the cabin?" She joined him at edge, peering over.

"Walking. Unless I can push it loose." He swung one leg over the side, sinking into the cold water. Drawing his other leg over, he hit the muddy lake floor. Waves lapped at his waist.

He pressed against the raised side near the stump, feeling the burn in his arms. But it didn't budge.

With one hand on the edge of the damaged boat—he was going to owe Marvin big-time, no way around that—Liam held out the other to Katie. "Coming?"

She stared at the murky water. "What's down there? Fish? Snakes?"

"Might be some of both, but I bet they're long gone. The boat probably scared them away."

Katie didn't take his hand. She remained frozen, her feet planted to the floor of the lopsided boat. "I don't like not knowing what I'm walking through."

He didn't either, but they couldn't stay here.

"I could carry you on my shoulders," he offered. "You'll never touch the water."

Katie nodded and looked up from the murky depths, taking his hand. Bending his knees, he helped her climb on.

"I'll come back for the bags," he promised once she sat on his shoulders, her knees bent and hooked under his arms.

With his hands on her calves, he stepped forward. He felt her fingers grip his short hair. "You won't drop me?" she asked.

"I've got you, Katie. Trust me."

Chapter 12

KATIE FOCUSED ON the cabin, the muscles in her legs flexing, gripping tight to Liam. They were halfway there, with the water lapping at his ankles, but he didn't put her down. He kept his promise, never letting her touch the water.

"We're almost there," Liam said, rubbing his hand over her calf. "You can relax."

She glanced down, feeling her leg muscles tremble. "I didn't want to fall."

"I'd never let you," he said, stepping onto dry land. He moved to the grass and crouched. "Ready to stand on your own two feet?"

Katie unhooked her legs and slid down his broad back. The feel of his body against hers pushed against the fear, demanding room for desire. *Stand on her own*—she'd been working toward that for so long. Ever since Liam had walked out of her life. But she wanted him back—for now, for tonight—and her reasons were as muddied as the lake water.

"I'm going to get the bags," he said. "Wait here."

He turned and waded into the water. When Liam was knee-deep in the murky depths, she withdrew her phone. She had every reason to call her brothers. She and Liam were stranded with their vehicles on the other side of the reservoir. She could ask Brody, Chad, and Josh to come for her, tonight, while she seduced the man who'd carried her to shore, asking for her trust. She could guarantee her brothers refused to give in to Moore Timber. She could stop Brody from making a stupid business decision because he thought it was in her best interest.

Her fingers moved across the screen, texting Chad, confirming that he would feed the animals as promised. She told him that she'd arrived at the cabin and was not sure when she'd be back. No mention of Liam or the boat stuck on a stump.

Liam returned to shore holding their bags and the groceries above his head. The muscles in his arms bulged from exertion, taut and tempting. But it wasn't the need to touch and explore the contours of his body that kept her from demanding her brothers rush out to the cabin.

Desire had a way of wrecking even the best-laid plans for revenge. And forgiveness followed close behind.

She'd spent seven years holding the past against him. But she was finding it harder and harder to cling on to the anger. He'd made a mistake. Violated her trust. And in the aftermath, she'd built walls to protect herself. Those barriers had taken years to construct. But she'd been taking them down brick by brick ever since he'd walked her home carrying her rescued goat.

Liam stopped in front of her, dripping wet from the waist down. "Ready to check out the cabin?"

Katie nodded, leading the way up the manicured yard to the structure that stood twice as large as any "cabin." The three-bedroom, log-cabin-style house featured a wraparound porch. At one end, under a covered gazebo, stood a swing covered in ornate pillows, and a pair of rocking chairs. In the center, the porch led to an expansive deck complete with a barbecue grill and seating for eight, maybe more.

She headed around the side, to the front of the house, and marched up the three steps to the door. A lockbox hung from the knob. Retrieving the slip of paper from her pocket, she entered the combination provided by the owner and found the key. She opened the door, stepped inside, and held it for Liam. He set the bags down, careful not to cross the threshold.

"Are you coming in?" she asked.

"I don't want to track water and mud through this place." Bending over, he unlaced his sneakers. "That rug you're standing on looks like it's worth more than anything in my house."

Setting his shoes aside, she watched as his hands moved to his waistband. The soaking wet fabric hit the deck, revealing his muscular legs. His T-shirt followed, leaving him in a pair of dripping wet boxer briefs.

Katie drew her lower lip between her teeth, taking in the defined lines of his muscular body. And his abs . . .

She wanted to reach out and run her fingers over him. Touch him. Taste him . . .

Logic told her to close the door. But her hands refused to obey. Out here, alone with Liam, feeling as if she'd left the past on the opposite shore, she couldn't look away.

"Is this your idea of foreplay?" she asked.

"Covered in lake water? No." He let out a low chuckle. "I'm going to take a rinse in the shower. When I get back, I'll start dinner."

He turned, walked down the steps, and disappeared around the side of the cabin. Maybe it wasn't his idea of foreplay, but the sight of his backside in those wet, clinging shorts? Katie slowly closed the door. She wanted to seduce him. But not in the shower. Liam desired a bed.

"In this place there has to be more than one," she murmured, picking up the bags. Setting groceries on the green marble kitchen counter, she scanned the expansive space. There was an island at one end, with three bar stools. The range top stood in the center of the space, attached to the island. High-end appliances lined the counters. The description had included a chef's kitchen, but she'd thought that meant it came with pots and pans.

Katie turned and headed down the hall. The first bedroom held a pair of built-in wooden bunks. She headed for the second and found a queen-size bed. Nice, but she had a feeling she could do better. Opening the third door, she spotted a bedroom set that belonged in a magazine. The room featured large timber pieces, including a four-poster bed covered in pillows and deep green blankets. It was like an island. And Katie had a feeling that once she climbed onto it she would never want to leave.

She set her bag down on wooden bench at the foot of the bed. Unzipping it, she withdrew the black satin slip with the lace trim. The store had labeled it a nightgown, but she couldn't imagine keeping it on that long. Stripping out of her jeans and shirt, she pulled on the fitted lingerie. The silky fabric grazed the tops of her thighs and dipped low between her breasts.

Barefoot, she padded down the hall and went in search of Liam. She heard movement in the kitchen. Standing at the island, his short hair wet from the shower, he wore a clean, dry pair of jeans low around his waist. The lines of his muscular abdomen dipped below his pants. She wanted to follow the path beneath his clothes, tracing it with her tongue.

He turned away, opening the fridge and reaching inside. "Hungry?" he called over his shoulder.

"Depends on what you're offering."

Closing the refrigerator door, Liam looked over at her. A slow grin spread across his face as he set a head of lettuce on the counter. "That outfit doesn't exactly scream, *I want a salad*."

"I had something more substantial in mind."

He crossed the kitchen and reached for the strap on her shoulder. His fingers toyed with the fabric. "We're stranded here."

She nodded as he traced the neckline of her nightgown, brushing the swell of her breast. Her nipples formed tight peaks that demanded more. "It's too late to call for help," she murmured.

He ran his hand up the other side, pausing at her collarbone. "We have all night. I could feed you first."

She reached for the front of his jeans, dipping her fingers below the waistband. "You could."

"Katie."

The rough edge to his voice sent a thrill swirling through her, settling in the places that craved his touch most. Holding tight to his waistband, she gave a tug drawing him closer. His powerful arms wrapped around her as his lips lowered to hers.

He kissed her, and every nerve in her body responded, begging for more. Releasing his pants, she hugged him tight, pressing every inch of her body against his. His tongue touched hers and she moaned. It was kisses like this that left lingerie decorating bedroom floors. And she would have stayed with her mouth pressed to his, waiting for the perfect moment to strip away the satin slip, if he hadn't broken away.

Liam leaned his forehead against hers, running his hands down her arms. "I want you so damn much."

"There's a bed down the hall." She entwined her fingers with his, stepping back and taking him with her. "A big one."

He moved with her, stealing kisses, running his mouth over her neck, her jaw, brushing her lips, as she guided them past the bunkroom, and the one with the queen bed. He stopped in the doorway to the master bedroom, his hands releasing hers, moving to her bare legs.

He drew back, his gaze fixed on the place where her black nightgown touched her thighs. "Is this what you planned to wear for your photo shoot?"

"No." She placed her palms flat against his chest, feeling the beat of his heart, pounding, racing. "Just for you."

His fingers stilled against her legs and he lifted his chin, looking down into her eyes. Without a word, he placed an arm at her back and the other under her knees as he swept her into his arms. He carried her to the bed and gently laid her down on the smooth green blanket.

"I'll be gentle," he said. "Take this slow."

No. She'd had gentle and slow. She didn't want either from him. She wanted the man who'd sparked her desire under the fir trees.

She shifted until she was kneeling on the bed, her knees spread as the nightgown rose higher. "Don't you dare."

"Katie." His brown eyes followed the hemline of her slip.

"I want *you*. No holding back." Bunching the black fabric in her hands, she stripped off the covering, revealing every naked inch of her. "Please, Liam."

He let out a low growl as he unbuttoned his jeans and pushed them down over his hips. He'd possessed an impressive body the last time she'd seen him stripped down. Watching him now, the hard, thick length of his erection jutting out from his body, she was left with only one question. Why had she waited so long?

"Lie down, Katie."

Her pulse raced. His commanding tone sent a thrill through her body, settling in the place that craved his touch. Seeing him stripped down had turned her on, but his words left her wanting and needing him.

She obeyed, lying back on the bed as Liam joined her. He straddled her, leaning forward to brush his lips over hers. He deepened the kiss before he pulled back, moving his hands to cover her breasts. She could feel every callus from his days spent felling trees. She waited for him to explore, for the rough touch of his palms to drive her sensitive nipples wild. But he kept his hands still.

Katie shifted beneath him, her body craving more while delighting in the way he held back, drawing out the wanting. But if he kept this up, she'd fight back, start making demands. "Liam—"

"Hands over your head," he ordered.

She drew her arms up, pausing when she reached her chest. Placing her palms over his, she guided his fingers, encouraging his touch. But Liam refused to follow her lead, instead lifting his hands up, his palms brushing against her nipples.

"More," she said, arching up.

"We'll get there. Trust me."

In this cabin, separated from their day-to-day by a lake? Yes, she trusted him.

"Place your hands over your head and keep them there," he said, staring down at her.

"Or else?" she challenged raising her one hand while keeping the other on his.

Releasing her right breast, he lowered his mouth to her chest and drew a circle around her nipple with his tongue. He stopped, lifting his head and meeting her gaze. "You will. I know you will."

Katie did as she was told, her fingers brushing the wooden headboard. He was right. She'd obey his requests without threats or ties binding her to the bed. She'd do it because the sound of his voice was like a caress, and the rewards for following his lead, pure pleasure.

He looked down at her, the expression in his rich brown eyes a potent mix of wicked wants and approval. Lowering his mouth again, he drew her nipple between his lips, sucking, tasting, teasing—and, oh heaven help her, *this* was what she'd wanted from him.

Keeping her arms over her head, her body writhed against the sheets, craving friction. "More," she demanded.

He drew his head back and raised an eyebrow.

"You're not the only one who can give orders," she said. "Not this time."

"Honey, in a few minutes, when you say 'more,' you'll be begging." Trailing kisses over her belly, he moved lower, shifting his body back. He guided her limbs apart, revealing the places he'd touched in the nightclub.

Positioning his broad shoulders between her spread thighs, he ran one finger up and down, taking a detour to draw a small circle around her clit. Katie lifted her head, watching and waiting for more.

Liam met her gaze with a wolfish grin. "I'm going to worship you. The only words I want to hear are 'more,' 'please,' and 'yes.' "

His tongue replaced his fingers, licking and exploring. Katie allowed her head to fall back, her eyes closing, losing herself in the sensations.

But then he stopped and she ground her teeth together.

"Do you understand?"

"Yes," she said, her voice heavy with the need coiling low in her belly.

With one hand, he parted her outer lips. He lowered his mouth and began to tease her, taste her . . . it was everything she needed and wanted from him. He lapped at her entrance, and her hips bucked against his mouth. Slipping one finger inside, his tongue returned to her clit. And, oh God, she was so close.

"More," she begged. "Please."

He gave it to her, pushing her further, until her body was like a rope pulled taut, ready to snap. His fingers slipped in and out of her as he drew his lips away. She moaned in protest.

"Come for me," he ordered. Lowering his mouth, he pressed his tongue against her, firm, demanding, leaving her no choice but to obey.

Her body snapped, breaking apart, her senses, her everything, overrun with pleasure.

"Yes, yes, yes!" she cried out, moving wildly, everything seemingly beyond her control as the orgasm raced through her. And then slowly, the explosive sensations faded.

Liam sat up, his hand still gently caressing her. "You're so wet. So ready," he murmured.

Hearing the promise of more in his words, she let out a soft moan. It felt as if she'd climbed up to a peak of pure pleasure, a place she hadn't visited in so long—and she wasn't ready to leave.

"Don't move," he ordered, his voice hoarse with desire as he disappeared off the edge of the bed. "Not an inch."

Through the aftershocks of her orgasm, she heard the rip of a condom wrapper and watched as he covered his impressive length. Then he returned to the bed, his body hovering over hers.

"I can't wait," he murmured, pressing against her entrance as his hands ran up her arms, his fingers interlacing with hers.

"Then don't." She lifted her hips to meet him, drawing him in. Closing her eyes, she felt him fill her. But then he stopped, holding his body still over hers.

"More," she demanded, wiggling beneath him.

"Honey, I don't want this to end. Not yet." But he did as she asked, moving within her, thrusting in slow, measured movements.

She squeezed her hands, letting him feel her nails. "Don't hold back. Please."

His gaze met hers and she saw the truth in his brown eyes. He was keeping a rein on his desire. He pulled back, releasing her hands, and rested on his heels. He wrapped his fingers around her leg, gently guiding her limb. "Roll over, Katie."

She did as he asked, shifting to her belly. Gripping her hips, he guided them up, positioning her on her knees.

She moved her hands beneath her shoulders, rising up on all fours.

Holding her, he slipped inside and began to move. This time, he didn't hold back. He claimed her. He made demands, no longer with words, but with his powerful body. Her fingers dug into the blanket, holding tight as she fought to maintain the position.

She felt his hand move between her legs, sending her spiraling into a second orgasm. Over the sounds of Liam moving against her in a now frantic rhythm, she heard moans, barely registering the sounds were coming from her.

"Ah, fuck," he growled, pushing into her one last time. His fingers never stopped, demanding that she come with him. She was so close . . .

And then the orgasm swept over her, swift and fierce. Lowering her head to the bed, she squeezed her eyes shut, not trusting herself to look back at him. As much as she wanted to close them out, emotions she didn't want or need here rode in on the waves of bliss. Being here, with Liam still inside her, felt like coming home to a man who knew her—to a man who ignited her wants and needs.

But he wasn't part of her plans.

Chapter 13

LIAM SLOWLY OPENED his eyes, his hands still holding tight to Katie. He didn't want to let her go, not until he saw the look in her eyes.

"Katie?"

She slipped out of his grasp, rolling over until her back lay flat against the blanket. But she didn't move to cover herself. Her cheeks were flushed as she stared up at him. But this time, it wasn't the look of a wide-eyed, innocent girl opening up her heart. The woman looking up at him knew what she wanted. She'd gone after it, demanding that he abandon the slow and gentle path.

He sat back on his heels, studying her, when all he wanted to do was wrap his arms around her and never let go. Shit, maybe this time he was the one with the love-struck look.

"You all right?" he asked.

Slowly pushing up on her elbows, she grinned at him. "What do you think?"

Before he could answer, she slid off the bed, heading for the attached bath, her every movement smooth and self-assured. "Don't answer that. If you don't know the answer, I think you should try again after dinner. I'll shower while you work your magic in the kitchen."

He chuckled, allowing her words to push against the tension. He was ready and willing to try again. He would spend all night learning what she liked, how she'd changed. After all, this was just foreplay . . .

Minutes later, after he'd pulled on his spare pair of jeans—choosing to skip the shirt and shoes—and retrieved his phone from his bag, Liam headed for the kitchen. He needed to shoot Marvin a quick text and let him know about his boat. He also had to arrange for alternate transportation, but he figured that could wait until morning.

Locating a cutting board, he removed the tofu from the fridge, opened it up, and dumped it on the plastic surface. He stared at it. When he'd grabbed the package at the store, he'd assumed he could toss it on the grill alongside his steak. But it looked like a bar of wet, crumbling soap. He didn't have the first clue what to do with it.

Down the hall, he heard the shower turn off. His mind abandoned the tofu, choosing instead to picture Katie reaching for a towel and running it over her naked body. He wanted to join her, dry her off, and toss her back on the bed. Forget dinner. He needed a second chance to prove the explosive connection between them ran too deep to walk away from—in and out of the bedroom.

She'd blown him away when she'd said those three little words: *Don't hold back*. Her fire and her passion matched his, stroke for stroke. But they couldn't spend the night in bed. He needed to feed her, care for her, and show her that he wasn't here just for sex.

He withdrew a knife from the block resting on the island and began slicing the tofu. He'd picked up wooden skewers to grill the vegetables. Adding squares of tofu—if it didn't crumble to pieces first—might work.

He finished with the soaplike substance and moved on to the vegetables. As he impaled the peppers and mushrooms on the wooden sticks, his thoughts shifted back to Katie. He'd given her every reason to keep her emotions under lock and key. He should have known she wouldn't turn to him, her expression filled with young love. She'd grown and changed. And hell, he liked the woman she'd become more and more. But he'd hoped for some sign that she felt the same pull he did.

Liam gathered the food and headed for the door leading to the grill. "I sure as hell hope she likes tofu."

"I do."

He glanced over his shoulder. With her wet hair framing her face, forming ringlets, Katie stood in her jeans and fitted green tank. She moved to the glass door, sliding it open.

"Need a hand?" she asked.

"I've got this." He wanted her to relax and let him take care of her.

"Want to grab a couple of beers and join me out here?" he added.

Just as he was setting the last of the skewers on the grill, Katie stepped onto the expansive back deck overlooking the yard. Facing due west, they had a kick-ass view of the sun dipping behind the coastal range on the far side of the lake. He could hear the water lapping against the empty dock, the sound blending with the crickets and the sizzle of the food.

Katie handed him an opened bottle of Oregon microbrew. "Nice view out here. I have a feeling Georgia will like this place. But I think I'm going to recommend that we hike in. It might mean some of the old friends I planned to invite won't come, but that could be for the best."

"The water level may rise by the time of your party," Liam said, using the metal tongs to turn the food from the grill. "But Georgia would probably prefer the hike."

He felt Katie move behind him, peeking over his shoulder.

"You didn't have to go to all this trouble," she said.

"For you? Yeah, I did." He pulled the skewers off the grill. "And you might want to hold your thanks until after you've tasted your dinner."

She walked over to the oval table and claimed a seat. Using a separate fork, he lifted his steak off, setting it on his plate. He put the dishes on the table and sat beside her. Raising his beer to his lips, he watched her take a bite.

"It tastes great, I promise," she said. "Now eat your dinner."

"Good." He reached for his knife and fork. It was nice to see her relaxed even if it was under the pretense of planning Georgia's party. "So, how are the horses?"

"Better." Glancing up from his plate, he caught Katie's lips form a soft smile. "The vet stopped by yesterday and said they need to gain weight. She also suspects one of them is blind. I'm trying to find a home for them at one of the nearby sanctuaries. But everyone is full right now. It is bound to get worse as winter approaches and people realize they won't be able to afford hay during the cold months."

"What is going to happen to your animals if you leave?"

Liam regretted the question, watching as she set the half-eaten skewer back on her plate. Now wasn't the time to talk about the future. But shit, the thought of her walking away from Independence Falls ate at him.

"Georgia told you," she said.

He nodded.

"I'm not sure. I'd like to take them with me. But it would be an expensive move. All the way to Montana."

"You don't sound too excited. The way Georgia talked about this Safe Haven place, it sounded like your dream job," he said, hoping Georgia had exaggerated Katie's desire to leave and work in another state. Liam knew she was passionate about saving animals, but she'd also invested a lot of time and energy into building her family's business. Part of him wanted it to be that simple. But he also had a feeling Katie didn't dream in the abstract.

"It is the perfect job. And I'm ready for Montana. I

could use a break from Independence Falls. I've lived here most of my life. Aside from the years I went to college. Even then I was only a short drive away. And my brothers used any and *every* excuse to come visit."

"I can see Chad eager to revisit college life."

Katie laughed. "He stopped by for the parties. But Brody and Josh? They came to check up on me. I'll admit, for a while I needed that. But now I want to be on my own and explore a new place. Make some new memories."

Deep in the pit of his stomach, guilt combined with dread. "Are the old ones really so bad?"

She didn't say a word. In the distance, crickets chirped and water lapped against the dock. But otherwise, silence. And he didn't move, needing to hear her answer before returning to his meal.

"Living in Independence Falls," she began, her voice so soft he was tempted to move his chair closer. "I drive by the place where my father ran off the road. He died there, in his truck, alone in the middle of the night. We'd just buried Granddaddy two days before. We'd known the end was near for him. But Dad? He survived his time in the army, fought overseas . . . We didn't expect him to have a heart attack at fifty-five. He was my daddy. And at eighteen, part of me still wanted to believe that he was invincible."

"Katie—"

"I was out that night," she continued, toying with her food for a moment before glancing up at the orange sky and the shimmering lake. "I took back roads home from town. If I hadn't, if I had taken the highway, I would have driven right past his rig. Maybe in time to help him. Get him to a hospital."

He pushed back from the table and held out his hand. They could finish their meal later. Right now, he needed to hold her, offer the comfort he should have given years ago. "Katie, come here. Sit with me."

She obeyed, rising from her place and settling into his lap. He wrapped an arm around her, wishing he'd pulled on a shirt. He'd been focused on teasing and tempting her back into the bedroom, not serious conversation.

"You can't think like that," he said. With his free hand, he touched her chin, guiding her head until her gaze met his. "It's not your fault."

"I know. But knowing I was so close during his last moments . . . I was minutes away from saying good-bye to him. I hate that I never had the chance."

Liam stared into her green eyes. He'd thought her bad memories of this town revolved around him. If he could win her forgiveness and make her see that this time would be different, that he wouldn't run, he wouldn't hurt her, then she would stay. But it ran deeper, so much deeper . . .

He interlaced his hand with hers as the arm snaked around her waist drew her closer. "I can understand wanting to escape those memories."

"Don't you think about leaving? A fresh start someplace that doesn't remind you of the people you lost?"

"I thought about it after my parents passed away. But Georgia was in school and she needed a place to come home to. So I started logging." He shrugged. "It's what I know. I grew up working in the forest, same as Eric."

He looked out at the lake. The sun was dipping low behind the mountains. It would be dark soon and the temperature would drop too. They should finish eating and head inside. But he couldn't let her go. Not yet.

"I told myself I would leave when Georgia graduated," he continued. "But then she joined the army. And I felt paralyzed. If I left, if I walked away from our hometown, what would she have to come back to? I needed her to come home. I couldn't lose her too."

He closed his eyes, feeling the weight of his words like the heavy fear he'd carried around day and night while his sister had been overseas. Katie squeezed his hand.

"Now this place is my home," he added. "My future is here."

Opening his eyes, he looked at their joined hands, resting in her lap. *Our future.* But he couldn't say the words. He couldn't tell her that running from memories didn't make them disappear. Look at Georgia. She carried hers with her across the ocean.

No, he couldn't use words. He needed to show her. Tonight. Before they left this place and returned to the other side of the lake. When they got back Independence Falls, the negotiations to buy her family business, the one her late father had nurtured and grown, waited for them. And when Katie learned of Eric's plan to hire her and bind her to Independence Falls?

His hand resting on her hip ran up the side of her body, drawing her closer. On Monday morning, when Eric presented his offer, she'd feel trapped. And there was no doubt in his mind, she'd look to him, accusing and demanding to know why he'd hadn't said a word about the deal during their time together.

Shit. He couldn't do that to her. He had to tell her. Now.

"Katie, honey, I want you to stay, but there is something you need to know—"

"I can't." She raised her hand, pressing a finger to his lips. "I can't stay, Liam. I want to be here. Tonight. With you. But I can't make promises beyond that. If that's not enough for you, I understand."

He turned his head, running his lips over her palm. He should tell her about Eric's plan. But out here, removed from Independence Falls, with Katie perched on his lap, the need to be with her, to love her, won.

"What did you have in mind?" he murmured, punctuating the question with a kiss in the center of her hand. They could discuss business in the morning. He silently promised they wouldn't leave the cabin until she knew about Eric's offer.

Katie broke free from his hold, sliding off his lap. "I think it is my turn to call the shots."

"And if I disobey?" he asked, watching as she returned to her chair.

"You wouldn't dare." In the near darkness, he saw her pick up her knife and fork. "But first, I'll let you finish your dinner. I'd hate for that steak to go to waste."

Yeah, that wasn't going to happen, he thought, hardening to the point that he might explode. The thought of Katie vying for dominance narrowed his focus to the here and now.

"Later." He stood, picking up his plate. "It's getting dark out here."

"I don't mind."

"I do." He picked up her dish and headed for the sliding glass doors. "You better believe I want to see the expression on your face when you make your demands."

If they had only tonight—and she'd better be prepared for the fact that he wasn't going to let her walk away without a fight—he wanted to spend it worshipping her, caring for her, giving her damn near all he had to offer.

Chapter 14

KATIE PAUSED IN the doorway. The things she'd revealed on the porch, she'd never shared with anyone, not even her brothers. How could she tell her family, the people who loved her no matter what, that living with them in Independence Falls left her second-guessing her past choices over and over?

But she'd told Liam, the man she had reason to distrust. On the porch, she'd been open and honest with him, proving once again that she'd pushed beyond her desire for revenge. She no longer held the past against him. But what did that mean for the future?

Katie shook her head. That question, the future—it didn't belong here in this moment. Right now, she wanted to focus on the fever pitch of need rushing through her at the thought of seducing Liam, of calling the shots.

She stepped inside, drawing the door closed. She watched as Liam placed their barely touched dinner in the fridge and turned to her. Everything about this man, from the way he stood, his bare feet planted hips' distance apart with his strong hands on his hips, to his sharp brown eyes, left her eager to walk into the moment and never look back.

"What do you want, Katie?"

She heard the challenge in his tone. If she didn't take control, he would. But she wasn't about to let that happen.

"You," she said, closing the space between them. She touched his chest and began tracing the outline of his muscles. "At my mercy. Calling my name."

She looped her fingers beneath the waistband on his jeans, brushing her thumb back and forth over the button. The head of his cock touched her fingertips and she could feel him straining for more. Moving backward, she headed for the overstuffed leather couch in the den area, pulling Liam with her. He followed willingly, his lips forming a smile that threatened to melt away her resolve and let him have his wicked way with her.

Stepping onto the soft rug, Katie paused in front of the couch. Using both hands, she undid the button on his jeans and lowered the zipper, freeing his erection. She wrapped her hand around him before stealing a glance up at his face. His jaw was tense and his gaze was fixed on her hand, watching and waiting. If she faltered, even for a second, he'd reclaim control.

Reluctantly, she released him and went to work removing his pants. "Sit down."

"Sure you don't need help with your clothes?" His voice was a low growl. The tone and timbre sent red-alert signals through her body.

"Sit down, Liam." She gave him a little push and waited until he'd settled into the cushions before sinking to her knees between his splayed legs.

"I want to be clear on the rules," she said, wrapping her hand around him.

"I'm listening," Liam murmured.

She lowered her head, running her tongue around him, ensuring she had his full attention. "Place your hands behind your head, grip the couch cushions if you want, but you can't touch me."

"And you think I'll agree to this because—"

She took him in her mouth, running her lips down to meet her hands.

"Oh hell yes," he hissed.

She lifted her head, but kept her hold on him. "And the second rule. The only words I want to hear from your lips are 'more,' 'please,' and 'yes.' "

Liam let out a strained laugh as she placed him on the receiving end of the command he'd issued earlier in the bedroom.

"Understood?" Her lips grazed the tip of his cock.

"Yes."

Katie licked him beginning at the base and he let out a low moan as his hips rocked up, demanding more. His sounds and movements left her aching for his touch. Re-membering his instructions from years ago, under the fir tree, she moved her free hand to her breasts, brushing the hardened nipple through the thin fabric of her tank top. She knew, just knew, he was watching.

"Oh fuck, Katie. You're killing me." He thrust up into

her mouth, harder and faster. But she stilled, gently lifting her head and looking him in the eye.

"More," he said, the smile on his lips in sharp contrast to the need in his brown eyes as he realized his error, and her determination to stick to her rules. "*Please.*"

Lowering her mouth, she took him as deep as she could, savoring his growl of approval. The hand touching her breast headed south. Having him at her mercy had her turned on to the point she couldn't hold back. If she didn't touch herself, she might abandon her plan, strip off her clothes, and straddle his lap.

Through her shorts, she pressed the heel of her hand against the part of her body demanding friction. She moaned, swirling her tongue around his tip, before taking him deep again. Her hand worked in time with her mouth.

She felt Liam's fingers in her hair, drawing her back. "Game over, Katie. You can call the shots later, I swear. But right now, honey, I need to taste you."

She heard the dangerous edge in his voice and was about to refuse even though his words sent a thrill down her body, when he added: "Please."

That one word—it was supposed to be a plea—but crossing his lips, it was a command. She released him, resting back on her heels.

"Please, take off your clothes."

"Since you asked nicely . . ." Reaching for the hem of her tank, she drew it over her head and tossed it aside. She rose to her feet and quickly stripped away the rest of her clothes. "Better?"

"Yes."

With a wicked smile that promised to make up for the fact that he was vying for control, he stretched out on the couch. The leather surface wasn't long enough for his six-foot-plus frame, but he didn't seem to give a damn.

"Come here, honey."

It took some adjusting, but Katie managed to straddle his face while taking him deep in her mouth. As he licked and kissed her, pushing her closer to release, she silently thanked him for breaking the rules.

This, she thought as she felt his hips thrust up into her mouth, *was so much better.*

His hands wrapped around her bottom, holding her still as his tongue swept across her sensitive flesh. Katie moaned, a low, throaty sound. If he kept this up, she'd explode.

She lifted her mouth, her hand never stopping. "Come for me. Now."

LIAM HEARD KATIE's demand and his body took over, begging to do exactly as she ordered.

"You first," he managed.

"No." He felt her struggling to hold back. But shit, with the way her mouth moved over him, she was going to win the battle.

"Please." But she took him so deep he felt the back of her throat, and he lost it, pumping his hips up, when he should have pulled back.

"Ah, fuck, yes!" he moaned, his fingers digging into

her backside. And then she followed him over the edge, crying out his name over and over.

Slowly, he sat up, pulling her into his arms, holding her close. He never wanted to let her go. But he had a sinking feeling he couldn't keep her. Katie amazed him— and it went far beyond sex. She knew what she wanted and went after it. Who was he to hold her back?

Liam closed his eyes, listened to her still ragged breathing. He'd walked away once because he had nothing to offer her. But this time, he had a feeling she would leave him in the dust. A piece of land with a view and a share of Moore Timber—he'd been foolish to think that she'd be drawn to those measures of success.

Yet his need for something tangible, to be able to say, *Yes I own that*, ran deep. He'd seen firsthand what happened to people whose lives were ruled by love. His parents had died within months of each other, madly in love until the end. But they'd lost their home, could not pay their medical debt, and left their children with limited options.

He felt her lips graze his chest, drawing him back to the present and the woman who'd just rocked his world.

"You all right, honey?" he asked.

"I feel so satisfied," she murmured. "I don't think I can move. My limbs feel like noodles."

"That good, huh?"

"Hmm," she said. "I should always be in control."

"We'll see about that." Rising off the couch, he scooped her up, cradling her in his arms. "For now, let's get you to bed. I have a few ideas of my own."

"OK," she murmured, looking up as she looped her

arms around his neck. "And then in the morning, we're going to explore your fantasies."

The part of his body that should have needed a lot more time to recover leapt at the thought. "That's one helluva promise to make to a man when you can barely keep your eyes open."

LIAM WOKE TO the first rays of sunlight pouring in through the windows and Katie pressed close to him. With her long hair spread over the pillow and her face against his chest, so close he could feel her breathing, she looked young and innocent, nothing like the woman who'd taken command of his body last night. He ran his fingers gently through her tangled curls. Her shower last night had destroyed her straight and sophisticated locks, but he liked her better this way.

Not wanting to wake her, he reached his free hand out and found his cell perched on the bedside table. As much as he wanted to keep her locked away from the realities waiting for them in Independence Falls, they had to find a way to get home. And there was the small issue of his friend's boat. Checking his texts, he found a message from Marvin. Help was on the way this morning. The message was sent in the wee hours, so Liam figured it would be late morning before they saw his friend.

Katie stirred beside him, opening her eyes and looking up at him. "Daylight already?"

"Sneaks up on you when you get to sleep late." He tucked a stray curl behind her ear.

"We need to find a way back to our cars."

"Done. I texted Marvin last night and explained the situation." He waved his cell before setting it on the bedside table. "He's coming to our rescue, but it might be a while."

"Enough time for breakfast?" She sat up, tossing back the covers and sliding out of bed. He watched as she slipped into her clothes.

"If that's what you're hungry for."

"Food first." She offered him a devilish smile before disappearing down the hall. "But don't think I've forgotten my promise. Even if it was made in an orgasm-induced haze."

He pulled on a pair of jeans and headed for the kitchen, feeling as if he was breaking the magical spell with every step. He found her by the coffeemaker furiously typing on her phone.

"Everything OK?"

"My brothers sent a barrage of messages last night, text and voice, demanding to know where I was." She poked the screen one last time and held up the phone. "This is why I need to move to another town. I told them I was safe and would be home in the morning. They don't need to know where I'm spending the night. I'm not twelve! I wouldn't have said anything to them if I didn't need one of them to check on the horses."

"Maybe something is up with the animals?" Liam opened the fridge and pulled out the orange juice and a carton of eggs. He knew better than to take her brothers' side, but he also had a little sister. He'd spent years worrying about Georgia. It was hell.

Katie traded him a glass of juice for a skillet. "No. They made it clear in their messages that the animals were fine. It was me they were worried about. And they had no reason."

No, the Summers brothers had every reason to be concerned. For all they knew, Katie had headed into the woods alone. If they learned she'd spent the night with him—the man who'd broken her heart years ago and now wanted to buy their company—they would throw punches first and ask questions later. He'd do the same in their shoes.

Liam lit the gas burner and set the pan over the flame. When he turned back, she handed him a bowl.

"For the eggs," she said. "I'll make the coffee."

They continued moving around the rented kitchen as if this was routine—breakfast together after a wild night of sex.

"Did you call them back and let them know you're OK?" he asked, pouring the whisked eggs into the pan.

"I sent Chad a text. He's the most reasonable of the bunch. Most of the time." She poured two cups of coffee. "Milk and sugar?"

"No thanks." He took the mug and returned his attention to the stove. But it was hard to focus while trying to figure out how to tell her about Eric's offer.

"Do you track Georgia's every movement?" she demanded, setting plates on the counter.

"That's Eric's job now." When his little sister lived with him, after her stint in the army, he'd tried.

Katie stared at him over the rim of her coffee cup. "You're as bad as they are."

"When it comes to my family? I'll take that as a compliment."

Her lips curled into a devilish smile. "How does it feel to be on the other side?"

Liam raised an eyebrow. "The other side?"

"This time you're the one giving them a reason to track me down. If they knew I was here, with you . . . well, I don't think they'd invite you in for a beer this time." Katie headed for the bar stools at the kitchen counter. "Might make it hard to close the deal. You're risking a lot by being here. With me."

Were her words a warning? He'd known that pursuing Katie might backfire. Had she taken that into account and made plans to blow up the deal?

Setting the plates down on the counter, he looked her straight in the eye. "I am. There's a lot on the line here."

"Am I worth it?"

He heard the challenge in her voice, underscored by a hint of unease. And he remembered something she'd said while walking home with her goats. Most of the guys she'd dated ended up hanging out with her brothers instead of her. This bold, beautiful, and stubbornly independent woman needed someone who would fight for her, risk everything for *her*.

"Yes."

Chapter 15

KATIE LEANED BACK on the stool, but didn't look away. She couldn't. Not with that one word hanging between them.

Yes.

Part of her couldn't believe she'd asked the question. Did it matter if he was willing to put his hard-earned success at Moore Timber on the line for her? Yes. He'd come after her when it would have made more sense to turn away. To risk so much, he had to be driven by more than desire.

Katie bit her lower lip, drawing it into her mouth. Maybe, just maybe, this man saw her for who she was, and who she wanted to be, and refused to walk away.

"I wouldn't be here if you weren't," he added, holding out a fork.

She took the utensil and poked at her eggs. Liam had a list of reasons to walk away from her, but instead, he'd come after her, refusing to give up. Of course, there was always the chance this was a ploy. She'd brought him out here intent on revenge.

She looked up, noting the way Liam studied her with his jaw set in a firm line. She believed in his yes. Somehow, they'd rebuilt the trust he'd shattered years ago. If they hadn't, she wouldn't have opened up to him last night, sharing pieces of herself she kept locked away.

And Liam had to know by now that she was not the weak link in the contract negotiations. If he was here, it was for her.

Part of her wanted to be *his*. But beyond these walls, it wasn't possible. This man was rooted in this town. If she wanted to be true to herself and her dreams, having him in her life was impossible.

Katie set her fork down beside her untouched eggs. Regardless of what waited for them on the other side of the lake, the fact that he was here now mattered.

"I'm not hungry anymore," she said, sliding off her stool. He watched her, his egg-filled fork raised to his lips. While she'd been lost in thought, he devoured half his plate. She smiled, turning to the door and reaching for the bottom of her shirt. "At least not for eggs."

She drew the T-shirt over her head and tossed it behind her, stealing a glance at Liam. He'd set aside his breakfast. The hunger in his gaze—it was for her. But he didn't follow her.

"Before we go there," he said, his tone low, rough, and downright needy. "There are things I need to tell you—"

"No. We only have a few hours before the outside world interrupts," she said. "Let's not bring it in here."

He shook his head. "Katie, you don't understand."

"Please." She knew that if this moment fell apart, if they turned the conversation away from desire and fantasy, they might never get back here again.

"I would hate to leave before I fulfilled my promise," she added.

Without waiting for a response, she headed down the hall, stripping off her jeans. She heard footsteps followed by a low growl of approval. Excitement pulsed through her as she stepped into the master bedroom and turned to face him. He'd abandoned his clothes in the hall and now stood before her naked and incredibly turned on.

And powerful—she could feel his energy from across the room. He was keeping it on a tight leash, one she wanted to snap.

"Right here, in this room," she said softly, slipping out of her underwear and tossing it aside. "I'm all yours."

He moved to her, reaching for her, running his rough palms over the curve of her waist, moving higher, skimming the sides of her breasts. She let out a soft moan. But he didn't stop. His hands moved to her shoulders and down her back. He paused when he reached her bottom, cupping and squeezing. Her breath caught as he lifted his hands away. The anticipation . . .

"Liam," she whispered.

His hands returned to her backside, brushing back and forth before lifting away again.

"Do you fantasize about taking me over your knee?" she murmured, looking up at him, taking in his heated gaze as her body warmed to the naughty image in her head.

"That's up there," he admitted, lowering his head and capturing her lips. She arched into his touch, running her tongue over his lips. He broke away, leaving her panting.

"I want to make you *mine*, Katie."

His words felt like a caress touching her breasts, running lower, down between her legs, leaving her wet and aching.

"Is that something you want?" he asked, releasing his hold on her and stepping back.

"I suppose I could play the bad girl."

Liam let out a low chuckle. "Yes, honey, you could. Now turn around."

She obeyed his commands, struggling to keep her breathing under control. She'd never allowed a man to spank her. With the way her body felt so close to coming, just from the promise of it, she wanted to try.

"Grab the bedpost," he ordered, his hands moved to her hips, drawing her back until she was bent at the waist. "You're sure about this?"

She turned her head, looking over her shoulder without releasing the post. "I like to read. I know that a woman can maintain her sense of self and still enjoy a spanking now and then."

His brown eyes widened. "What the hell are you reading?"

"And I have a feeling you'll like seeing your mark on my backside," she said, ignoring his question.

"Yes."

She drew her lower lip between her teeth before

turned away from him. "We won't know if I like it unless we try."

He pressed his palm against her before lifting his hand away. Without a word of warning, he brought it down, smacking her bottom.

It didn't hurt. And she knew it sounded worse than it felt, but still, she looked back at him, her eyes wide with surprise and something that felt an awful lot like I'll-hurt-you-if-you-try-that-again. She'd expected a rush of pleasure like she'd read about in books, but instead he'd erased any feelings of wanting and desire.

"Did that turn you on?" she demanded, still holding the bedpost.

"Honey, you're looking at me like you don't want me to touch you, so no." He moved closer, reaching for her again. But this time his touch was soft and gentle. "I want you melting in my arms, begging me for more, and screaming my name when you come."

"That sounds like a much better fantasy." She walked her hands up the bedpost, arching her back until her nipples almost grazed the wooden surface. Her feet moved closer and he followed, keeping hold of her.

His palm moved to her heated bottom. "We could always try it again," he teased. "Just to be sure."

"Don't you dare!" Laughing, she stepped out of her reach, pulling her body flush against the bedpost before turning to face him.

"OK." He held his palms up in mock surrender, his shoulders shaking as he fought to hold back his laughter.

"Katie?" A deep, familiar male voice called from beyond the open bedroom door. "Are you here?"

"Her car's not out front." The sound of the front door closing punctuated the sentence. "But someone must be here. There is a plate of eggs on the counter."

Her laugh died. Her brothers had found her.

Liam's teasing smile vanished as he moved to the door, drawing it shut. "Sounds like we have company."

She nodded, looking around for her clothes. But they weren't there. She'd left them scattered throughout the cabin . . . for her brothers to find. Katie closed her eyes. She'd sought revenge. She'd been eager for her siblings to find out she'd been with Liam. But she'd moved past that plan, choosing to forgive, to set the past aside and enjoy this moment with Liam, and still her siblings had found out. Or they would in a moment, unless she and Liam escaped through a window and made a run for their broken-down boat.

Probably not the best plan.

She opened her eyes, watching as Liam pulled a pair of jeans out of his bag. Moving to her overnight bag, she grabbed the first pair of shorts and T-shirt she could find. She needed to get out there and talk to her brothers before they searched the place.

"I didn't ask them to come," she said, keeping her voice low. "I don't know how they found me."

He zipped up his jeans, his hands moving to his hips. "I didn't think you had."

His faith in her cut like a knife.

"I need to get out there." She drew her T-shirt over her head and moved past him, heading for the door. "Wait back here and I'll send them away."

"No." His hand closed around her biceps, drawing her to a halt. "I'm not letting you face them alone."

"They're my brothers," she protested. If they saw Liam, they'd start talking with their fists.

"You go out there and I'll join you in a minute. They're going to figure out you're not alone. We left plates out and clothes."

She nodded. "You're right."

"I'm guessing they probably would be more pissed off if you had come out here by yourself without telling anyone." He released her arm and she moved to the door.

"And Katie," he called after her. "This time, I'll follow your lead."

She paused, her hand on the doorknob. She could hear her brothers on the other side, searching the cabin, muttering to one another.

"You trust me to handle this?" They'd been here before. Well, not *here*, exactly. Her brothers hadn't almost walked in on Liam spanking her seven years ago. But close. "To handle them?"

"I do."

"Katie?" Brody's voice boomed through the cabin. Judging from the sound, her brothers were close to the master bedroom.

She quickly opened the door and slipped into the hall, careful to keep Liam hidden from view. "I heard you, Brody," she called, walking into the open kitchen/living space.

Her brothers turned at the sound of her voice, drawing together to form a line of tall, imposing male bodies. Her oldest brother's eyes were bloodshot, as if he'd been up most of the night. All three looked a little rough around the edges with their untucked shirts and worn jeans. If she hadn't known them forever, she might have been intimidated.

Katie crossed her arms in front of her chest. "I wasn't expecting you."

"We've been looking for you half the night," Brody said. "You can't disappear without a word about where you're going."

"And who you're with," Chad added nodding his head toward Liam's discarded jeans.

"Yes, I can," she said, looking first at Brody, then Chad. Josh had moved off, heading for the sliding glass door. "I'm not a little girl. You can trust me to take care of myself. And I did send a text letting you know when I'd be home."

She looked from one stern, pissed-off brother to the next, refusing to give an inch. "Now, if the three of you are here, who fed the horses this morning?"

"Georgia offered when I called to see if she'd seen you," Chad said.

"Is that your boat stuck out there?" Josh asked, his tone more curious than angry. "Looks like you would have needed help sooner or later."

"Someone is coming," she said.

"Marvin?" Chad said. "We ran into him last night in town. At close to three in the morning when you didn't respond to my calls. Marvin said he'd lent his boat to a friend who wanted to visit this side of the lake. Drunken old fool wouldn't say who."

She heard the bedroom door open and wondered if Liam had been waiting for the right moment to make his entrance. She didn't turn around, instead watching her brothers' expressions turn dark and foreboding.

Chad's hands formed tight fists, his eyes widening. "Shit, is that—"

Liam stepped into the open area and moved to her side, placing a hand in the small of her back. His touch proclaimed, *She's mine*, loud and clear. And left her wondering if he'd meant what he'd said, if he would follow her lead.

"Hey guys," Liam said. "Were you out hiking this morning?"

Chad stepped forward, his eyes darting to the discarded jeans, the two plates of eggs, then back to Liam. "I'll give you five seconds to explain what the hell you're doing out here with my sister."

"And if your reasons have anything to do with Moore Timber's offer," Brody added, his voice low. "You're going to have a hard time swimming back to dry land."

LIAM ADJUSTED HIS stance, bracing for a punch while forcing a smile. Brody was right. Liam deserved to take a hit. He'd come here for Katie, but the fact that he hadn't told her about Eric's proposed offer made him a bastard.

Katie quickly stepped in front of him. It took all his self-restraint not to pick her up and move her out of the path of flying fists. Not that her brothers would take a swing at Katie, but still, he wanted to fight this battle for her.

"Back off, Chad," she ordered. "And Brody, not another threat. This has nothing to do with Moore Timber."

"Katie," Liam said. But this wasn't the place to tell her. Not with her brothers looking as if they wanted to take him out.

She glanced back at him. "I've got this."

Liam wanted to eat his words. He should never have promised to let her handle Brody, Chad, and Josh. Winning her trust now, in this moment, wouldn't matter when it broke into pieces at Monday's meeting.

"Please," she added before turning back to her angry siblings. "I invited Liam. We're planning Georgia's bachelorette party."

Liam pressed his lips together and nodded. Her brothers stared back at him with a trio of slack-jawed expressions.

"Georgia had a list of ideas and Liam volunteered to help me scout locations," Katie continued. "I thought it might be fun to include Eric and his friends. You know, a Jack and Jill party."

"Would you have his and her strippers?" Chad asked.

"No strippers," Liam and Katie said at the same time.

"Just hiking out to the cabin," Katie added. "Maybe spend some time on the water."

Brody eyed him, before focusing on Katie. "I wish you'd said something. We were worried. More so when we heard about the boating accident."

"We hit a stump," Katie said. "And I know how to swim, Brody. You taught me."

"Did you stay in separate rooms?" Chad demanded.

Liam glanced at Katie, ready and willing to let her handle that one. Chad was a big boy and he'd probably already guessed the answer. Or maybe he thought they'd run through the cabin tossing their dirty laundry around for fun.

Katie put her hands on her hips. "You really want the details of my sex life?"

"Ah, hell," Josh muttered from his corner by the window.

All three brothers glared at him.

"No." Brody looked away first, shaking his head. "Let's get out of here. We'll wade out to the boat and see if we can get it off the stump while you pack up. Liam, you're coming with us."

"I should give Katie a hand with the dishes first," Liam said. He needed to talk to her alone.

Katie turned, smiling at him. "Don't worry. I'll clean up in here. My brothers will probably need your help with the boat. They're not as big and bad as they look."

"Christ, Katie, if taking that job in Montana means you'll move out," Chad muttered, "I'm starting to think it's a good idea."

As far as confrontations with Katie's brothers, this

one was a helluva lot better than the last. But whether the Summers brothers took a shot at him or not didn't matter, he realized. Katie trumped them. Gaining her trust and winning her heart came above everything else—because he was pretty damn sure he'd handed over his.

Chapter 16

WITH A STATION wagon filled with three sulking men, Katie turned onto the main road and headed for the other side of the lake, where her brothers had parked their truck. They'd been furious to find her at the cabin with Liam. And spending hours waist-deep in the lake freeing the boat hadn't elevated their moods.

"I wish you'd let me drive," Brody said from the passenger seat.

"From the sounds of it, I got more sleep than the three of you," she said.

"I doubt that," Chad muttered from the backseat. "I still can't believe you spent the night with Liam Trulane. Again. You were a mess after the last time. What makes you think this time will be any different?"

"I'm older and wiser." *And because she would be the one walking away.* "You don't have to worry about me falling apart when it ends. In fact, it is already over. Last night was a one-time thing."

"Did he tell you that?" Brody asked, his voice low and intent.

"No. That was my choice."

"Katie," Josh said. "I hate to be the one to ask, but are you sure this thing between you two wasn't about the sale?"

"Yes." She smiled. "Yes. He has more to lose than I do. For all he knows you're so pissed you'll refuse to take the meeting tomorrow."

"Sis, I'm angry," Chad said. "But I'm not walking away from millions of dollars because you're messing around with a guy who broke your heart once. Like you said, your choice."

As if her so-called revenge plot needed another hole.

"He did start coming around right after Moore Timber made an offer," Brody said. "He's the friend who took you barhopping the other night, right?"

She nodded. "I wasn't lying when I said he's helping with the bachelorette party."

Pulling up beside Brody's truck, she put her wagon in park and turned to her brothers. "This isn't about the deal. I swear. Georgia told him about the potential job in Montana. And I guess he wanted to see if there was something between us before I left."

"Is there?" Brody demanded.

Yes. Something hot that spoke to her desires and awakened her fantasies. One night with him had left her feeling wanted, worthy, and oh so special.

"No," she lied. "But he makes great eggs."

"Both plates were full when we arrived," Josh pointed out.

"That's not his only talent," she said, turning her attention to the backseat.

"Katie." Chad ran his hand over his face, while Josh stared out the window. "Please, no more."

Brody opened his door and placed one foot on the ground outside before turning to her. "If anything changes, come to us, Katie. We're your family and we're here for you. Got that?"

"Yes. And even though I hope you guys don't spend another night looking for me—you were fools to do it this time—thank you. But I'm fine. I've got this. And I want you to promise me you won't do something stupid, like start a fight with Liam because of last night."

She paused, but they didn't say a word. "I need to hear you say it. My life, my choices. You don't get to throw punches because of them."

"Promise," Brody grumbled. The others nodded their agreement.

"But I still don't trust him," Chad said, opening his door.

"You don't have to, Chad. I do," she said softly. "I trust him."

KATIE POUNDED ON Georgia's front door as the setting sun turned the sky three shades of pink. Her long, twisted day—waking up to Liam, the confrontation with her brothers, the trip back to shore once Marvin arrived to tow the damaged boat—was behind her. But Liam's words, the way he'd let her handle her brothers, had left her feeling as if she'd stumbled onto a cliff, uncertain if the ground beneath her would hold. She'd put on a strong front for her brothers, but after she'd dropped them off, the brave façade had crumbled.

Right now, she didn't want or need more uncertainty in her life. She couldn't allow the ground to fall away, leaving her hurt at the bottom. She had too many questions in her life right now. Should she accept the job in Montana? And what about Summers Family Trucking? Would she be able to keep the company for Brody?

Liam Trulane was just one more question mark in her life.

"Georgia?" she called, knocking a second time. "Are you home? We need to talk."

Katie needed help sorting out her L-words. After everything that had happened in the past twenty-four hours, she feared that she couldn't be trusted to think clearly. And there was the small issue of the bachelorette party that was now a coed event.

The door opened and the largest golden retriever Katie had ever laid eyes on greeted her. Behind the dog, whose body blocked the entry to Georgia and Eric's home, stood a thin blonde with waist-long, wavy hair, wide blue eyes, and a heart-shaped face. In her long, flowing sundress, the stranger looked as if she'd walked out of the pages of a magazine.

"Hi," she said softly, carefully positioning her body

behind the dog. Her free hand brushed the retriever's soft coat. "Georgia's upstairs putting Nate to bed. She'll be right down. Please, come in."

The woman stepped back, holding the door wide open, and the dog moved with her, staying close by her side. Katie walked past her, turning when she reached the open foyer to offer her hand. "I'm Katie."

"Lena. It's nice to meet you," the other woman said, silently refusing the handshake.

Letting her hand drop to her side, Katie felt the retriever pressing against her legs as if trying to physically move her away.

"And that's Hero," Lena added. "He doesn't let anyone get too close."

Katie nodded, piecing the information together. Lena was the friend from Georgia's PTSD support group. And Hero was the dog who would attend the bachelorette party at his owner's side.

Georgia appeared at the top of the stairs and quickly made her way down. "Perfect timing! Nate's asleep. Now we can enjoy a drink on the patio and talk about your wild adventures last night. Your brothers nearly hauled Eric out of bed at three in the morning to hunt for you."

Katie shook her head, following Georgia into the kitchen. Lena and Hero trailed behind them. "You know, this is your fault."

"I don't take responsibility for Liam's actions." Georgia opened the fridge. "Beer or wine?"

"Wine," Katie said, moving to the cabinet that held the glasses.

"Lena?" Georgia asked.

"If you're sure I can spend the night, I'll have a glass," the quiet blonde said, her fingers once again trailing over Hero's coat. "I can always drive back to Portland. Find a hotel. One that accepts dogs this time."

"No. You can stay here as long as you like." Georgia pulled out a bottle, twisted off the cap, and began pouring. "As long as you promise to help with the wedding planning."

Lena smiled. "Thank you."

"At this rate, you might need to help Katie with the bachelorette." Georgia handed Katie a glass. "I got an earful from my brother about stupid party ideas."

Katie took a sip as they headed for the sliding door that led to the expansive blue stone patio, pausing for Georgia to pick up Nate's monitor. "Your brother wasn't a fan of the photographer."

"Photographer?" Lena asked, settling into a chair. The golden retriever sat at Lena's feet, his gaze fixed on her as if he wasn't sure yet if he could trust her to steer clear of his mistress.

Georgia explained her idea for the boudoir photo shoot.

"I can't imagine letting a stranger take pictures like that," Lena murmured, her eyes widening. "Not that I have anyone to share them with anymore."

"It doesn't matter now." Katie sipped her wine as she stared at the setting sun. It had slipped lower behind the mountains, leaving the sky a rich orange. "Liam vetoed the idea."

"You weren't supposed to tell my brother," Georgia said. "But don't worry, I have a few new ideas."

Katie groaned and closed her eyes. "Please tell me you didn't Google bachelorette parties again."

"No. I think you're right. The top ten lists don't fit me. But I still want a party. I'm getting married and I don't want to miss a chance to celebrate. So I was thinking, what if we invite the people who have been there for me since I returned home? Just enough to make it feel like a party. We could have it here. Fire up the grill."

Katie opened her eyes, turning to her friend. "I love it. Now, how would you feel about making it a coed event? Included Eric, Liam, their crew from the company, my brothers—"

"If they promise not to kill Liam," Georgia said.

"They won't," Katie said firmly. "I won't let them."

"But it sounds like they have a good reason to take a swing at him." Georgia waggled her eyebrows. "After what happened at the cabin?"

"I don't kiss and tell," Katie said, borrowing the line Georgia had used when she'd fallen for Eric.

"Please, I don't want details." Georgia raised her hands, palms out. "He's my brother. But you like him, don't you?"

Katie stared at the pond separated from the back patio by a slope of well-maintained lawn. The smooth surface shimmered in the fading light. They were back to L-words. And when it came to Liam, she had a list.

Like? Check.

Lust? Check.

Love?

Katie took a long drink, draining the rest of her wine. This time around he'd given her every reason to believe in him. He'd said all the right things, making it so hard not to fall madly and deeply in love.

"I do," she said softly. "But what I feel for him doesn't matter."

"Montana is not that far away," Georgia said. "Maybe you don't need to end whatever it is you've started."

"You could ask Liam to go with you." Lena's soft voice startled Katie. She'd almost forgotten about Georgia's new friend and her dog. But now Katie turned to her.

"There is nothing written in stone stating his dreams come before yours," Lena added, her tone growing stronger with each word.

Katie shook her head. "His home is here. It's a lot to ask—"

"Giving up on what you believe in, on your hopes and dreams, that is a lot to ask too." The golden retriever stirred at her feet, resting his head in his owner's lap.

"Sorry," Lena said. "I don't know your situation. And I'm hardly one to talk about relationships. Hero is the only male who had gotten close to me in the past six months."

Georgia sighed. "You're going to steal my brother away, aren't you?"

"Maybe," Katie said. "After tomorrow's meeting, once the deal is out of the way, then maybe I'll ask him."

And see if Liam would stand behind his words and risk everything to be with her.

"I think he'll say yes," Georgia said. "I know my brother and he doesn't go after anything he doesn't want."

Katie's smiled as she stared out into the darkness. The last traces of daylight had disappeared behind the mountains.

"Then bring on the L-words."

Chapter 17

KATIE SECURED SUGAR's stall door. When she'd returned home, she'd gone straight to the barn to check on the animals. They'd been fed and watered. Now, the shower was calling her name.

Walking down the barn's center aisle, she stole one last glance at the pair of horses the sheriff had dropped off. They'd confirmed that the smaller of the two half-starved mares was blind. But still the mare had adjusted to her new home, happily eating her way through buckets of grain and bales of hay.

Katie paused in front of the blind animal's stall. "I should have brought you a treat."

"I have a carrot I don't mind sharing."

She jumped at the sound of his voice, startling the mare. The skittish horse quickly moved away. Glancing over her shoulder, Katie spotted Liam, one shoulder resting against the opening to the barn, his left ankle crossed over his right. He'd changed into a clean pair of jeans and a flannel shirt, the sleeves rolled up, revealing his forearms. His hands were shoved into his pockets.

"Liam." She smiled, wishing she'd stopped by the house to clean up before checking the animals. "Hi."

"I saw the light on in the barn and thought I'd find you here." He abandoned his position in the entry and headed for the mare's stall.

"Didn't bother checking at the main house? I'm sure my brothers would love to see you again," she teased.

"I had to see you, Katie." He withdrew a carrot from his back pocket and handed it to her. The nervous mare came forward to accept the treat, then quickly disappeared into the far corner of her stall.

"I'm done here. And while I'd love to sneak you into the house, there's an apartment over the barn that is empty right now," she said. Liam didn't need to see her pink and purple wallpaper.

"I came here to talk. There's something I should have told you at the cabin. But I was too damn selfish. And then your brothers showed up . . ."

And just like that, the cliff she'd been standing on started to crumble. She took a step back, crossing her arms in front of her chest, her chin held high. "Tell me."

"One of the guys at Black Hills called and told us about your deal with them."

"So this is about Moore Timber's offer," she said. Her brothers' warning raced through her mind. Had she been a fool to trust this man a second time?

He nodded. "Eric and I agree that Summers Family Trucking is worth more than one million—".

"Eric said yes to the counteroffer?" Surprise mingled with unease. "And you didn't tell me?"

"Katie," he said. "Listen to me. Eric is willing to increase the offer. A lot. But he has one condition."

"You mean you have one condition," she said. "You're part of Moore Timber now. Eric's partner, not just his spokesman."

"You're right. We want you to come work with us and help Moore Timber gain a foothold in the biomass space. The way you've negotiated that deal—you did a great job, Katie."

"I know." Her brothers hadn't believed her at the time, but she'd been right to take the risk. "You're one of Summers Family Trucking's biggest assets," Liam said. "We want your fleet of trucks, don't get me wrong. But we also want you."

It was like watching a series of dominos fall. Her heart, her plans for the future were tumbling one by one. And the man who'd shattered her trust years ago was pushing them over.

WHEN KATIE HAD first looked at him, Liam had nearly turned and walked back to his truck. The expression on her face—he'd seen it before, in a clearing under a pair of fir trees. Love bound tightly with hope shone in her bright green eyes. Only this time she wasn't an eighteen-year-old who'd just lost her virginity to a man who didn't deserve her. She was a strong woman who knew her own mind—and this time, he was asking for so much more.

"Is this your way of trying to keep me in Independence Falls?" she asked, her open, loving expression now covered with a mask of suspicion. He had a feeling that hurt lay beneath, but she refused to let him see it.

"No," he said, his voice firm. He needed her to understand that last night at the cabin, their trip to the nightclub—it wasn't about closing a deal. He'd wanted to return to that moment when she trusted him with her heart. He'd wanted to prove that this time he wouldn't run away.

"If this, us, was all about the deal, I wouldn't be here now. I would have let you walk into that meeting tomorrow without a heads-up about Eric's counteroffer. Hell, from the standpoint of a guy who wants to keep his job and his best friend, I shouldn't be here, telling you. But I couldn't let you walk in there not knowing."

"Thank you," she said evenly.

"I went to the cabin with you because I wanted to give you a reason to stay that had nothing to do with contracts," he said. "I know you have bad memories of this town. I know you're tired of living under your brothers' watchful gaze. And believe me, honey, I get that. But would it be so bad to stay? You'd have a great job and you could afford to keep your horses. I'll build you a new barn, more fields on the land next to yours. Think about it, Katie, your family is here. I know they're annoying, but believe me when I tell you that you're going to miss them, headaches and all, when you go."

"Liam, you can't just walk back into my life, offer me a job and a place to keep my animals, and expect me to say yes." Her surprise had given way to anger and he could hear it mounting with every word. "It's not that simple."

"I know Katie. I know." He ran his hands through his hair. "Whatever you decide Katie, it's your call. You can say no to the offer. I'm not trying to make this choice for you. This is up to you and your brothers."

He turned around, heading for the door. Eric would be pissed when he found out that Liam had talked to her before tomorrow's meeting. But he didn't care. For years, he'd chased success, but now he'd toss it aside for her.

Liam paused in the door, looking over his shoulder at Katie. He'd always thought of her as his, but he'd been wrong. Katie Summers had a hold on his heart. He belonged to her. And he'd realized it too late.

Longing, sadness, regret—it was all there in his brown eyes. She stared back, replaying the conversation in her head. She'd mistakenly assumed that if he asked her to stay, it would be for him. But no, he wanted her to remain in Independence Falls because she was smart and a valuable piece of Summers Family Trucking.

She hated the thought of setting aside her plans for a man who'd broken her trust once. But there was so much more to consider here. Her brothers, their future, and *millions of dollars*.

It was too much for tonight. Tomorrow, she would

make a decision. Her choice. By coming to her tonight, Liam had made that possible.

"Liam," she called. The one thing she knew for certain right now? She couldn't let him walk away. "Wait."

Liam turned in the entryway and she went to him, taking his hand in hers. "Thank you for telling me. I would have felt ambushed, walking into that meeting to-morrow, if you hadn't come here."

He nodded.

"I'm not making any decisions tonight," she said. "Except for one. I'd like you to stay."

"Katie," he murmured, running the pad of his thumb over her cheek. "Are you sure?"

"Yes. No matter what happens, I want to spend to-night with you." She led him out of the barn, switching off the lights, and headed for the side door leading up to the apartment.

Bending over, she found the key under the rock beside the door. Then she moved the rock to the other side of the entryway.

"Is that your signal that someone's here?" he asked, his voice lit with humor.

"Yes, but they can't get in without the key." She un-locked the door, turned on the stairwell light, and led the way up. "Brody has the master, but he rarely if ever uses this place."

At the top of the stairs, she opened the door that led to the small, clean studio apartment. A double bed stood on one side opposite a small kitchenette, which held a mini-fridge, toaster, and coffeemaker. They'd talked about renting the place for extra cash at one point, but Chad and Josh had voiced strong objections.

Setting the key beside the toaster, she faced Liam. "We started something this morning before we were so rudely interrupted."

He raised an eyebrow. "You want another spanking?"

"No." She shook her head. "But I'm guessing that's not your only fantasy."

He chuckled, crossing the small space, and gathering her in his arms. "Honey, when it comes to you, I have a long list."

Her fingers toyed with buttons on his flannel shirt. "What's on the top?"

"Look at me, Katie."

She obeyed, freeing the first button and moving to the second. But watching his smile fade, her hands stilled. The weight of the emotion in his deep brown eyes nearly stole her breath away.

"I want to make love to you," he said, his large, strong hands cupping her jaw. "Let me love you tonight, Katie. That's all I ask."

She nodded, no longer trusting her voice. He stared down at her for another heartbeat before lowering his lips to hers. Through a whirlwind of needy kisses, their clothes fell away. His hands were everywhere, touching, caressing, and driving her wild as he guided her to the bed.

"Lie down, Katie."

Again she obeyed, willing to give him anything here, tonight. His gaze swept over her and he let out a low growl, followed by a curse.

"I wasn't planning to stay," he said. "I didn't bring anything."

She blinked as he joined her on the bed. His body covered hers, hovering above her, his weight on his elbows as his kissed her collarbone.

"I don't have a condom, Katie." His lips moved to her breasts, heading south. "I still want to make love to you, but I can't—"

"In the nightstand," she gasped, as he shifted off her and fumbled with the drawer. Turning her head, she watched as he withdrew an unopened box and tore into it. He quickly covered himself and returned to her.

Katie smiled, welcoming him back into her arms. "You don't need to rush. We have all night, Liam. All night."

But beyond that? Katie closed her eyes, pushing the question away, choosing to focus on the man loving her as if this night meant everything—as if it was all they had.

Chapter 18

LIAM WOKE TO the smell of coffee and a beautiful naked woman standing beside him. "Hey."

"Morning." She smiled down at him, but it didn't reach her eyes. "You phone has been ringing on and off for a while. I think you overslept."

"Shit. What time is it?"

"Eight."

"Yeah, I need to get going." Liam pushed back the covers and retrieved his cell from his pants pocket. Glancing at the screen, he saw half a dozen messages from Craig, one of Moore Timber's crew chiefs.

"There's a problem at one of the harvest sites," he said, pulling on his pants. Buttoning his shirt, he looked up at her. She'd dressed and stood sipping a cup of coffee. "I hate to run, but this is important. The mechanical harvester isn't working and if that's not running, we'll fall behind."

"And time is money in timber," she said. "I know. Go. I'll see you later. At the meeting. You'll be there?"

"I'll try," he said. He walked over and gave her a quick kiss. "This isn't good-bye."

She nodded, but didn't say anything. Part of him wanted to stay and draw a promise out of her that whatever happened, this wasn't the end. But his phone buzzed with another text and he knew he needed to leave.

In his truck, Liam pulled out his cell and dialed as he buckled his seat belt. A minute later, he steered his truck down the Summers driveway with his phone pressed to his ear. He sped past Chad's truck, pulling up the drive, and offered a wave.

"Hello?" his best friend said after three rings.

"You can't make this deal contingent on Katie." Liam turned onto the main road headed out of town. "I won't be at the meeting this morning. There's a problem at the harvest. But I'm telling you, restructure the offer. I told Katie about it last night. I couldn't keep it from her."

"When I heard you two had run off to a remote cabin for the weekend, I had a feeling that might happen," Eric said. In the background, Liam heard his friend's nephew trying to trade a toy dinosaur for a second serving of maple syrup. "She didn't go for it."

Eric sighed. "I can't just give them millions of dollars without some promise that Katie will stay and help us at least transition her relationships. I can give her options. But Liam, she might not like them."

"She's not going to agree to stay, man, I'm telling you."

Liam said, slowing down, knowing he would lose cell service soon.

"I thought you were going to work your magic," Eric said. "Convince her to be your girl."

"It didn't work that way." Liam tightened his grip on the wheel. "I swear, man, Katie fucking owns me, body, heart, and soul—the whole deal."

"Ah, hell," Eric said. In the background, Georgia admonished him for swearing.

"At least I have another reason to hire her," Eric added. "She can boss you around."

KATIE SMOOTHED HER knee-length black pencil skirt as she followed Brody and Chad into the Moore Timber conference room. She'd paired it with a white button-down shirt and a low heel that felt foreign on her feet. She stumbled, but regained her balance before falling onto the carpeted floor.

Chad smirked at her. "Tired from another late night?"

"Not at all." She pulled out a chair at the large oval table and sat.

Chad selected the seat beside her and leaned close. "Liam was pulling out of the drive when I got home."

"You're not the only one who can use the apartment over the barn," she said, turning away from her brother to face her friend's fiancé. Seeing Eric at the head of the table in a three-piece suit left her fidgeting in her seat.

"Josh won't be joining us today," Brody said from his

position at the opposite end of the oval table. "One of our drivers called in sick, and he agreed to fill in for him."

Eric nodded. "Then let's get started."

Katie drew a deep breath, interlacing her fingers in her lap. She'd debated telling her brothers what Liam had shared with her last night, but they'd both been away from the house this morning. Brody had been out fixing a truck and Chad was just returning from his latest fling.

And part of her wasn't sure what to say. She still hadn't decided what to do.

"Liam was called away too, but I spoke with him this morning. We would like to offer you three million for Summers Family Trucking."

Beside her, Chad let out a low whistle.

Eric smiled. "As part of the deal, we'll keep your drivers at their current rates."

"Thank you," Brody said gruffly.

"Brody—" Katie said.

"I'd like to hear him out, Katie," Brody said.

"We'd like you all to become part of the Moore Timber family. Brody, we'd like you to manage the day-to-day," Eric said, and her oldest brother nodded. Eric turned his attention to her and Chad. Katie tensed, but Georgia's fiancé wasn't looking at her. Yet.

"Chad, Liam told me about your interest in helicopter logging," Eric continued. "Moore Timber has been looking to invest in a chopper. We'd be willing to work out a deal on the start-up cost and hire you."

"Wow," Chad said. "That would be . . . thanks. That would be great."

One look at her brothers' expressions—even Brody was lit up as if proud of the number Eric had assigned to the business he'd worked so hard to build and maintain—and Katie knew she couldn't walk away from this deal. Life had not handed the Summers family much. But Eric Moore was offering to unlock the doors to her brothers' dreams.

"Josh has already been picking up shifts with us," Eric said, turning his attention back to Brody. "We're happy to hire him on full-time."

"We appreciate your generous offer," her oldest brother said, and she could tell by his tone that Brody was waiting for the catch.

Eric's smile faded. "For the three-million-dollar price tag, we would need to include a contract for your biggest asset."

"Sure," Chad volunteered.

"We would need Katie to commit to two years, with the potential to extend," Eric said.

Katie released the breath she'd been holding while Eric explained why her relationships and the contract she'd negotiated—the one her brothers had dismissed—made Summers Family Trucking worth millions.

"And if she says no?" Chad asked, his smile slipping away.

"If Katie is not interested, well, I'm afraid our offer drops." He turned to her. "I strongly feel that without Katie the Black Hills contract will disappear and the relationships will deteriorate. I'm not exactly the go-to guy in the biomass arena."

"I'm surprised you're interested in it now," Brody said, the brief hint of excitement that fate might finally rule in their favor erased from his expression.

"I still believe it is best for the forest floor to let the branches decompose. It keeps the soil healthy for the next crop of trees," Eric said. "But I also think it pays to be forward thinking. Biomass has the potential to replace coal as a form of energy to a certain extent. Overseas we're already starting to see this happen. I think it could be good for the timber industry at home too."

"And you need Katie for this?" Brody asked.

"Those relationships are in their infancy," Eric said. "You purchased the trucks to haul the wood product a month ago based on your financials. So yes, we do."

"We'll take the deal," she said.

Her brothers had given up a lot for her. It was her turn now. She couldn't walk away from three million dollars just because it was not part of her dreams. If this is what they wanted, what Brody felt was the right next step . . . Her family came first.

"Wait a minute, Katie," Brody said. "You were planning to leave. Move to Montana. Start a new job. Run your own sanctuary."

"I can still go," she said, forcing a smile, telling herself this was her choice. "In two years."

Brody frowned. They both knew barns filled with needy animals wouldn't wait. Carol Lewis would hire someone else to replace her as the head of the Montana Safe Haven.

"We'll talk it over." Brody pushed back from the table

and everyone else followed his lead. "And have an answer to you in the morning. I'd also like to review those contracts."

Eric walked around the table and handed her brother a stack of papers. Then he turned to her and held out his hand. "Welcome to the team. I hope."

The door opened and Liam stepped in. She felt his gaze taking in her fitted skirt and button-down shirt. He stared at her hand clasped in Eric's and his expression darkened. She bit her lip, wishing they could return to the moments last night when the outside world hadn't mattered.

"What did I miss?" Liam demanded.

"I said yes," she said. "It's done."

Liam's jaw tightened. "Katie, can I have a word with you?"

She nodded, fighting to keep her polite smile in place as she followed him down the short hall to his office. Apart from a desk and two chairs, one covered with chainsaw safety gear, the space was empty, as if he hadn't bothered to move in yet.

She glanced out the window. Liam had a view of the parking lot. As an equity partner, if that's what he got, she had a feeling her office would stare a wall.

Liam closed the door. "Katie, are you sure about this? It kills me to think you felt trapped, that you had to take his offer."

She did, but not by him. "You know, the funny thing is, before you came over last night, I thought I'd solved my problems. I thought that I'd found a way to make my dreams come true and still have you in my life. I was going to ask you to come with me. To leave behind your job and Georgia—"

"Yes."

She shook her head. "I made my choice."

"You haven't signed the contracts," he pointed out.

"We will," she said. "We will."

He heard the hint of sadness in her voice. It was as if the spark that burned bright inside her had been extinguished. And God, it was killing him that he'd had a hand in stealing away her dreams.

"You shouldn't have to sacrifice your plans for your brothers," he said.

"They've given up a lot for me," she said. "And no one walks away from three million dollars, especially when someone is offering them everything else they want. Even Brody can't say no to the deal Eric offered."

Liam waved his hand toward the closed door. "Do you think they are still here?"

She nodded. "They'll wait for me. Chad is probably hitting on your receptionist. Now that he officially works for Moore Timber, you better warn your female staff. He is Mr. One-Night Stand."

"If they're still here, go get those contracts and tear them up." He closed the space between them, looping one arm around her waist and drawing her close. "Take the job in Montana. I'll go with you. Together, we'll save horses, goats, whatever you want."

"I can't," she said. "You didn't see their expressions when Eric said the number, or when he agreed to help

Chad buy a helicopter and outfit it for logging. If my dad were alive, he'd be so proud. And wait until Josh finds out he finished his last haul. He hates driving trucks. Now he can go back to school, work for Moore Timber, whatever he wants."

"Did you even try to negotiate with Eric?" Liam demanded.

"No. At the end of the day, family is more important. And who knows, in a few years, I'll probably be glad I'm not living in some unfamiliar town, responsible for hundreds of animals no one wants to adopt." She offered a forced smile. "Not all dreams come true."

"No, Katie," he murmured lacing his fingers through her hair, running his thumb down her cheek. "Don't say that."

He wanted her to live her life unguarded, going after what she wanted, finding happiness, one lonely and abandoned animal at a time. She wasn't his to keep. He knew that now. He'd betrayed her trust twice, and still she continued to believe in him. She'd blown him away last night when she'd taken him at his word, trusting that he hadn't tried to set her up. But that didn't mean he couldn't put her first.

A plan formed in his mind. It might backfire or fall apart. Hell, maybe he was crazy. But he had to try. For too long, he'd been so afraid of failing—Eric, the company, his sister, Katie—that he hadn't stopped to think that letting this deal crash and burn might be part of loving Katie.

"I'm not going to let you give up," he said. "I love you,

Katie. I want to be the guy who makes your dreams come true, not the one who shuts them down."

He lowered his lips to hers, kissing her, quickly deepening the connection. She moaned against his mouth and he drew her flush up against his body. He knew what she liked; the places to touch that would leave her screaming his name. With one palm pressed against her back, he ran his free hand down her neck. With his fingertips, he gently traced the V-shaped neckline of her button-down shirt.

He wanted to dip low between her breasts and undo the buttons. But that wasn't part of his plan. And he didn't have much time. Leah, their receptionist, would only entertain Chad Summers for so long.

Moving his hand over her shirt, he held on to her hip as his mouth kissed a path over her jaw, down her neck. Her moans grew louder without his lips covering hers. Katie pulled at his flannel shirt, freeing it from his jeans. But when her fingers began to toy with the buttons, he stepped back, capturing her wrists in his hands.

"You're so damn beautiful. I want you so fucking much." He looked into her green eyes, burning bright with desire as her lips formed a sweet smile. One look and he knew this was worth a shot.

Holding her wrists with one hand, he touched her cheek with the other. He drank in the sight, memorizing it, knowing that in a moment, it would break apart.

Liam claimed her mouth, his kiss hard and demanding. His free hand roamed over her curves. She struggled against his hold, but he held tight. He deepened the kiss, savoring the taste and feel of her, the way her body pressed up against him.

Katie moaned as he trailed kisses over her jaw, down her neck.

"More, Liam," she begged. "Please."

Using his body, he guided her back until her thighs pressed against the edge of his desk. "I wish I could bend you over my desk and lift your skirts."

"Liam." She arched, trying to press up against him even though he still held her wrists tightly between them. "*Please*. Don't hold back."

"Katie?" Brody's voice echoed in the hall. A second later, the door to Liam's office swung opened.

"Let her go," Brody demanded.

Liam stepped away, releasing Katie's wrists as her brothers filled the cramped office space, confirming two things. Liam's office walls were way too thin.

And those contracts? In a few minutes, they'd be history.

CHAPTER NINETEEN

herself.

Chapter 19

KATIE FELL BACK against the desk. She'd been so lost in
Liam's kiss, in the way he'd held her as if he never wanted
to let go, that she'd forgotten for one brief moment that
her brothers were nearby. She steadied herself just in time
to see Chad grab a fistful of Liam's shirt with one hand,
drawing his other back to take a swing.

Scrambling, and nearly falling over thanks to her
stupid heels, she grabbed on to her brother's arm. "You
promised, Chad."

Katie turned her attention to Brody. "You too."

"We did." Her oldest brother nodded to Chad. "Let
him go."

"You've got to be kidding me!" But Chad did as he
was told, releasing Liam. Katie exhaled, feeling a rush of
relief.

"You have every right to take a swing," Liam said.

"Don't goad them," she hissed, looking at him.

"Oh, I want to," Brody said, his tone leaving no room for debate—he meant what he said. "Still, we did promise Katie. If she wants to do whatever you two were doing, we won't stop her."

"It won't happen again," Liam said. "You have my word. It's over."

"What?" Panic rose as she turned to Liam. He didn't mean those words. He wouldn't walk away from her. Not again.

"Good-bye, Katie," Liam said.

She placed her palms flat against his chest. "You're not walking out of my life. Not this time."

Liam shrugged. "The deal's done, Katie."

"Liam," she gasped. Those words felt like a slap to the face. He couldn't mean them. He'd said he loved her. He'd made promises—

"No." Brody stepped forward. Raising the contracts, he tore them in half. Opening his hands, the pieces fell to the floor. "No way in hell am I giving my blessing for my little sister to work for you. What you do behind closed doors is your business, Katie. But I'm not signing a document that requires you to work for him."

"Katie, I'm with Brody on this," Chad said. "You shouldn't be bound by some contract to work for this guy."

"They're right," Liam added.

Katie stared at the pile of papers on the floor and then up at Liam, the motivation behind his words crystalizing in her mind. "Chad and Brody, wait in the hall."

Chad shook his head. "Not this time."

"Yes. Leave the door open if you insist." Her brothers relented, moving just outside the doorway, never once looking away from Liam.

"You did this on purpose." Katie stared into his deep brown eyes, which still shone with the love he'd professed before setting her up. "You wanted to give them a reason to walk away. Are you crazy? This deal—it was in Moore Timber's best interest, your best interest!"

"Honey, when are you going to get it?" Liam smiled ruefully. "I want what is best for *you*. Always. I have from the beginning. Now you're free to take that job in Montana."

The way he'd faced her brothers all those years ago, knowing it would end in a fight, how he'd brought them to this moment when she tried to sacrifice her hopes and plans for the future . . .

"Oh Liam, when are you going to understand, you can't decide that for me." She glanced at the two imposing men hovering in the hall and raised her voice. "None of you can."

Chapter 20

KATIE STEPPED ONTO Georgia's blue stone patio and slowly approached Lena, who was reading a book with the ever-present dog, Hero, at her feet. Katie was tempted to rush over, ranting like a crazy person. After the meeting and the scene in Liam's office, she felt as if she wouldn't be able to hold back much longer. But she didn't want to send Lena into flight mode, not when she desperately needed to talk to Georgia's new friend.

"Lena?" she called when she was ten feet away.

Both dog and owner looked up.

"Marie said I would find you out here," Katie said, referencing Eric's longtime housekeeper. "Do you mind if I join you?"

"Sure." Lena offered a tentative smile. "But Georgia's not here. She has an event at Nate's preschool, followed by a playdate at the playground in town. I don't expect her back until dinnertime."

"I was hoping we could chat. I could really use a friend today who doesn't know Liam, Georgia's brother, very well. Are you planning to stay in Independence Falls?"

"I'm not sure yet," Lena said, her fingers playing with the cover of the paperback she'd been reading. "I don't have anywhere else to be at the moment. Portland—it doesn't feel like home anymore. I gave my ex the house in our divorce. He has friends nearby and a job. It made sense."

Katie drew her legs up under her, settling into the cushioned lounge chair. "Do you have family? Siblings? Brothers?"

"I do. But they're not exactly in my life right now."

"Good for you. Brothers are a pain. Trust me." Quickly, before it sank in that she was pouring out the intimate details of her life to a virtual stranger and her dog, Katie told Lena the history of her relationship with Liam up to and including this morning's incident at the Moore Timber offices. Marie interrupted briefly to bring out a tray of lemonade. But by the end Lena was staring wide-eyed into her cup.

"I'm sorry," Katie said at the end of her saga. "You don't know me. Or Liam. But, well, what do you think? I mean, he told me he loved me and walked out of my life. Again. And he had the gall to tell me he was doing it for me! I always dismissed the guys who just wanted to hang out and have a beer with my brothers. But after today? They're probably a safer bet."

Lena nodded, reaching down to pet Hero. "But you don't love the other guys."

"I didn't say I love Liam," Katie clarified.

"I know." Lena stood and Hero rose with her. "Wait right here. I'll be back."

A minute later, the woman and her dog reappeared with a bottle of tequila and a bag of chocolate chips.

"A long time ago, before, well, everything," Lena said with a soft smile, "my girlfriends and I would get together for tequila whenever one of us needed relationship advice."

Katie cocked her head, studying the bottle. "Did it work?"

"Sometimes." Lena held out her hand for Katie's lemonade glass. "May I?"

Katie handed it over and watched as Lena poured the lemonade into the grass. Dog at her side, she filled the glass with two, maybe three shots. Then she set the bottle on the ground and reclaimed her chair.

"You're not having any?" Katie asked.

"No." Lena shook her head. "The chocolate chips are for me. I'm not much of a drinker anymore."

Katie took a long, deep sip, feeling the burn in her throat. "I like your friends," she said as the liquor spread through her. "Where are they now?"

"They're with my ex. In Portland. He got them in the divorce too."

"Some friends," Katie muttered, taking another sip.

"I think it was easier to understand his side of things." Lena reached for Hero, petting his coat. "He spent six months trying to make it work with a woman who didn't want to be touched. And until I got Hero, I never left the house. It made for a difficult marriage. And hurt a lot of friendships."

"I'm sorry."

Lena shrugged, opening the bag of chips. "I'm moving on."

"Maybe that's what I need to do," Katie said. "Move on. From Independence Falls. From Liam. I should probably call the owner of the Montana Safe Haven right now and accept the job."

"Is that what you want?"

"I . . . I'm not sure." Katie turned, looking out at the lake. "But I think I need to do it. Leave. Just when I was starting to trust him, Liam goes and pulls a stunt like today in his office."

"I don't think it is your ability to trust Liam that is the problem." Lena poured chocolate chips into her hand. "I think you don't trust yourself to stay true to your goals when you're with him."

Katie raised the tequila to her lips, tilted her head back, and drank—every last drop. The liquor scorched her throat, but she didn't care. "You're right. But I've been burned before."

"I can't help you there," Lena said. "The only male I allow to get close to me has four legs and, right now, some very bad doggie breath."

Katie laughed as Hero looked up at his owner. "I think you might be on to something. At least he's devoted to you."

"True," Lena said, popping a few chocolate chips into her mouth. "But after what you've told me, I think Liam's devoted to you. I think it is up to you to determine what you want. And if your dreams include Liam, go after him."

"He's betrayed me twice," Katie said softly.

"Betrayed? That's a strong word. I believe he's tried do what he thinks is best for you even if it breaks his heart."

Katie stared at the mountains. "He broke mine too."

The door leading to the kitchen opened and Katie turned, expecting to see Eric's housekeeper.

"I thought you might be here," her big brother said. He shoved his hands in his pockets as he crossed the blue stones to the sitting area. Brody nodded to Lena and Hero. "Hello. Brody Summers."

Hero and Lena stood, the dog moving in front of his owner, his gaze fixed on Brody. "Lena. Nice to meet you," Lena said, clutching the bag of chocolate. "I should go in and let you two talk."

Lena and the golden retriever disappeared into the house. Brody claimed her seat. Resting his forearms on his thighs, her brother leaned forward.

"I'm sorry, Katie," Brody said. "I don't have the right to make decisions for you. I just wanted what's best for you. Always have. This time, well, I thought that was the job in Montana."

"Have you stopped to consider what is best for you?" Katie demanded. "You gave up so much to keep our business running after Dad died. Maybe it is our turn to sacrifice for you."

Brody shook his head. "I didn't give up a thing."

"You could have moved away. Instead, you worked so hard to pay my college bills. You—"

"Enough, Katie. I'd planned to take over the trucking company long before Dad's heart attack." Brody stood and started pacing back and forth in front of her. "Taking care of you and Chad and Josh was not a burden. You're my family. As far as I'm concerned, you don't owe me a damn thing."

"Yes, I do," she said softly, her gaze fixed on the empty glass in her hands. "I want you to keep the business you worked so hard to build."

Brody stopped in front of her. "Katie, look at me. You accused me of making decisions for you. But walking away from this deal because you think it is what I want— you're doing the same damn thing."

Her eyes widened as she stared up at her brother. Turning the words over in her tequila-addled mind, she realized he had a point. They'd both been so damn concerned with making sure the other got what they wanted out of life.

"I want to sell to Moore Timber," Brody continued. "The deal Eric offered today . . . I'll get to stay on and the company will be stronger."

"You tore up the contracts."

Brody looked away, running his hand through his hair. "In the heat of the moment, seeing you with Liam, knowing that bastard hurt you once, yeah, I did. I would have preferred to slam my fist into his face."

"I'm glad you didn't," she said.

Brody nodded. "He was trying to do the right thing. But you're correct, we don't have the right to decide that for you. Whether you take the job with Moore Timber or move to Montana—that's your call. But whatever you decide, promise me that it will be what you want."

"I promise." She stood and wrapped her arms around her big brother, hugging him tight. "But first, I need some time to think."

"And more tequila?"

Katie looked up at her brother. "Maybe. But it probably won't help me make life-changing decisions."

"Probably not." Brody released her and picked up the bottle. "But you don't have to decide anything today. Take your time. Figure out what is in your heart."

Liam.

His name felt as if it had been tattooed on her soul. But how many times could she choose him knowing that when she offered her love, he might hand her back heartbreak?

Chapter 21

LIAM REACHED INTO the bed of his truck for his chainsaw and safety gear. Tossing the chaps over his shoulder, he turned to his Saturday afternoon project—limbing Marvin's trees. After all that happened in the past week, it felt a helluva lot like penance.

"There you are!"

Liam turned and spotted his sister marching toward him.

"I didn't realize you were looking for me." He set the chainsaw down. "Everything OK?"

"Josh Summers was working with Craig's crew today," Georgia began, struggling to catch her breath. It sounded as if she'd run down from the main house on the property to the wooded area.

"That's right. I saw him on the list I handed off to Craig yesterday." Without the three-million-dollar payday, the Summers brothers still needed extra work. Liam felt guilty about that, running the deal into the ground. But he'd talked to Eric about getting the brothers back to the negotiating table—this time without Liam involved.

Knowing he'd failed—that stung. But handing his freaking heart over to Katie, and let her walk away with it, hurt a helluva lot worse.

"Josh had an accident," Georgia said, ripping him from his thoughts.

"What kind?" Liam picked up his equipment and headed for his truck. "Shit, I knew the kid was pushing hard, driving trucks five days a week and working with our crews on weekends."

Georgia rushed to keep up. "It wasn't his fault. They were helicopter logging on the site. The pilot got sloppy and that big metal hook, the one that hangs down to carry the trees?"

"Yeah, I know the hook," he said, tossing his gear in the back. "Get in and I'll drive you back to your car."

"That hook hit Josh in the head." His sister opened the passenger door and slipped inside. "He's at the hospital now in critical condition. Eric went over to meet Brody and Chad there. But no one has seen Katie."

Liam had witnessed his share of logging accidents. But a large metal hook to the head sounded pretty damn serious. He turned the truck around and drove as fast as he dared over the dirt path to the house. "Have you tried her barn? The horse trails?"

"Her car was parked at the house and I checked the barn. Sugar was missing, but I didn't have time to search the trails. I came looking for you, figuring I'd reach

Katie on her cell. But she's not picking up. Have you heard from her?"

"I haven't spoken to her in days. Last I heard of her, Eric said she was passed out drunk at your place following Monday's meeting. She hasn't returned my calls. And her brothers sure as hell won't let me near her."

He pulled up to a stop beside her truck and Georgia hopped out. "I have to go pick up Nate, but then I'll keep looking."

"I'll find her," he said. "Keep calling her cell. I have an idea where she might have gone if she was on horseback."

Liam hightailed it down the driveway. If her brother was in critical condition, Katie needed to get to Josh's side. She already beat herself up over not being there for her father. If she didn't get a chance to say good-bye to Josh—if it came to that—she'd never forgive herself. And she'd probably run as fast as she could away from Independence Falls. As much as he wanted her to follow her dreams, he didn't want her to leave for the wrong reasons. Heartbreak held tight—and it was a lot easier to face surrounded by friends and family.

"KATIE!"

She heard his voice and opened her eyes, staring up at the tree branches. Sugar, who'd been tied to the tree happily grazing, glanced over at her.

"Katie!"

This time, she sat up, reaching behind her and brushing the leaves out of her long, straight ponytail. About twenty feet away, she spotted Liam racing toward her. He'd called every day since she'd walked out of his office. But she hadn't called him back yet. Her big brother had been right, she needed time to think.

She'd taken a long, hard look at her goals, setting aside her stubborn determination and focusing on what was in her heart. Saving animals, but also this place, this town, her family—and Liam.

Katie ran through her checklist of L-words every day while staring up at the twin fir trees.

Like? Check.

Lust? Check.

Love—

"Katie, you need to come with me. *Now*," Liam said, bursting into her quiet bubble under the trees.

She frowned, crossing her arms in front of her chest. This man might be the love of her life, but that did not give him the right to make demands after he'd walked out on her.

"Josh was in an accident," he continued. And just like that her frustration slipped away. Liam offered more details, but all she heard were the words "Josh" and "accident" over and over. "He's in critical condition. We'll know more when we get to the hospital."

"Critical condition," she repeated. Those words tied to her brother . . . no, this couldn't be happening. She couldn't lose him.

"Ride Sugar back to the barn," Liam ordered. "Fast as you can safely go. I'll drive my truck around and meet you there."

She nodded, numbly mounting Sugar. Liam placed a hand on her calf before she steered the mare to the path.

"Are you OK to ride?" he asked.

She nodded.

"Just get Sugar into her stall. Georgia will stop by with Nate later and take care of the animals."

He'd made arrangements, thought ahead when all she could think was *Josh* and *accident*. "Thank you."

"I'll get you there," he said. "I promise. Focus on riding."

Katie followed his instructions, racing off toward her property, pushing Sugar as fast as she dared. How long had Josh been at the hospital? When did the accident happen?

The questions she'd forgotten to ask swirled in her mind as she steered the mare home. When the barn came into view, she spotted Liam jumping down from his truck. He rushed to meet her, helping her remove the tack and close Sugar in her stall.

Liam took her hand, leading her to the truck. "Georgia will be here soon. I spoke to her on my way over. Do you have your phone? She has been trying to reach you."

"I left it in my room." She'd been worried she would be tempted to make a call before she'd thought things through. She turned away from the truck, but Liam caught her hand, pulling her back.

"If anyone needs to reach you, they can call me," he said, helping her into the truck and fastening her seat belt. "I'm not leaving you, Katie."

DAYS LATER AS fall started to take hold, Josh had still not opened his eyes. He was breathing on his own. They ran tests that showed signs of brain activity. The doctors debated how to classify his vegetative state. Sometimes he responded to stimulus, but most of the time he didn't move. By day seven, it became clear that the doctors here did not have all the answers. And there was nothing to do but wait.

Staring out the window of the cafeteria, Katie realized she'd spent twelve to sixteen hours a day at the hospital since Liam rushed her over. He cared for her all week, managing her animals and her life so that she could be here with Josh. He'd stepped up and helped her brothers, finding drivers to cover shifts and speaking with the mills regarding deliveries.

For the last week, Liam had put her family first. She'd never needed someone so much. And he'd been there, every step of the way.

"Katie? Can we join you?"

She turned away from the window at the sound of her oldest brother's voice. Brody and Chad carried a tray with three cups of coffee and a selection of cellophane-wrapped muffins.

"Here." Chad set a muffin in front of her. "You need to eat."

Katie reached for a cup of coffee. "Have the doctors finished their rounds yet? Liam dropped me off this morning, but when I went to Josh's room, they kicked me out for rounds."

"Yeah, they're done. I spoke with them. There is no change," Brody said. "But they are talking about bringing in a specialist from either New York City or Dallas. Someone more experienced with traumatic brain injuries. They said that could take weeks."

"Weeks. But won't he be awake by then?"

"Maybe," Chad said. "They don't know. The doctors are labeling Josh's condition a persistent vegetative state. There is no timeline. Trust me, I've asked every nurse for more information. No one seems to know a damn thing."

"What do we do?" she asked. "Just go back to our lives and wait?"

"Yes." Chad said. "We can take shifts here, but staying at his bedside 24/7 is not helping anyone. You look like you haven't eaten a real meal since the accident, sis."

"We also need to discuss the deal with Moore Timber." Brody sipped his coffee and nodded to the pile of papers to her right. "Eric is pushing for an answer. Frankly, I think it is because he knows we need money to cover Josh's expenses. Insurance doesn't cover everything. Not even close."

"Sign the contracts," Katie said firmly. She pushed the pile of papers across the table and offered her brothers a pen. "I want to work for Moore Timber. I've already called Carol at Montana's Safe Haven and let her know I can't take the job. I'm not leaving Independence Falls."

Her goals had shifted and changed. Josh's accident was part of it, but she'd made the choice before that, while lying under the fir trees. She'd chosen to rewrite her future. Sitting here, staring out the hospital window, she'd realized that Liam had been right. She couldn't escape her memories by moving to another state. Her life was here. Her family was here. Life was too short to waste chasing dreams somewhere else when happiness and love were right in front of her.

"And Liam?" Brody asked.

"I'm not leaving him either." She stood, taking the cellophane-wrapped muffin with her. "Call me if anything changes?"

Brody nodded. "Go get him."

"We'll stay away," Chad added. "Promise."

Katie drove to the Moore Timber offices and marched past reception down to Liam's undecorated office, clutching the signed papers. She found him staring at his computer.

"Hey," she said.

He looked up. "Hi. Everything OK? How's Josh?"

"No changes." She stepped into the office and closed the door. "But I brought you these."

"The contracts?" he said, pushing back from his desk and taking the documents.

Katie nodded as he rose from his chair, tossing the papers on his mostly cleared desk.

"You're staying?"

"I am," she said. "But not because we need the money or for my brothers. I'm not giving up on us. Not this time."

"Honey, that doesn't mean we need to stay here. If you want to move and take your dream job, we'll go."

She shook her head. "My dream is right here. My animals, my family, and you. I love you, Liam. I've loved you for a long time. Even when you ran from it, even when I was too stubborn to admit that maybe handing over my heart wasn't such a bad thing. And I have faith that you're not going to walk away from this."

"Never going to happen again. I was a fool to go the first time, thinking that success meant land and a fancy office job. None of that matters without you. My parents did it right, Katie. Love comes first. I'm in this forever. You're mine, Katie."

"Yes." She brushed her lips over his in a sweet, gentle kiss.

"And I'm yours, honey."

Epilogue

KATIE CARRIED THE last of the empty platters inside. They'd gone through all the hotdogs and burgers she'd purchased for the occassion. Yesterday, after weeks in a coma, her brother had finally opened his eyes. Josh was a long way from a full recovery. And the doctors still planned to bring in a specialist. But he would recover. The fear that had been hovering over her family and friends had lifted. Eric and Georgia had stepped forward, offering to host a casual, friends and family barbeque to celebrate.

"I've been looking for you." Liam's arm snaked around her waist, drawing her back to his front. His mouth nuzzled her neck, trailing soft kisses over her jaw. "Are you heading to the hospital?"

"No. Brody said he'd stop by and check on Josh. I saw him this morning," she said, leaning against him. "I need to go home. Lena asked if she could stay in the apartment over the barn and I agreed. She wants to give Georgia and Eric some space. With Nate visiting his grandmother, Lena felt as if she might be in the way."

"You told her where to find the key?" His lips touched her ear.

"I did. But I want to check on her. See if she needs anything."

"She'll be fine."

"I don't know. I saw Chad talking to her earlier with Hero positioned between them. I turned away for a minute, and when I looked back, my brother was covered in beer. As in someone poured it over his head. And I doubt Lena did that. She wouldn't get that close. Then the next time I saw Chad, he was with another blonde."

"Honey, I'm sure Lena survived her run-in with your brother. You can quiz her on the details tomorrow. But tonight," he said, drawing her earlobe between his teeth, then releasing it. "Tonight, I have other plans for you."

Her pulse sped up. "Maybe a detour . . ."

"Good." He released her, leaving her missing the full body contact, and took her hand. "I'll drive. We can come back for your car in the morning."

Ten minutes later, Liam steered his truck onto the shoulder of the two-lane road. Even shrouded in darkness, Katie recognized this place—the same spot where he'd found her trying to change her tire.

She climbed out, her eyes adjusting to the dark night. Clouds filled the sky, obscuring the stars. There was just enough moonlight to see Liam grab a sleeping bag and backpack.

"I wasn't expecting an overnight campout," she said.

Liam handed her a flashlight. "Surprise."

With the wide beam illuminating the way, she took his hand and headed through the woods to the familiar clearing.

"I should have waited for a starry night," he said. "But I wanted to come here one last time with you."

"Last time, huh?" She watched as he spread out the sleeping bags. He set a second bag down, retrieving a bottle of champagne and two plastic cups.

"Yeah. I listed the place for sale, back when I thought you were leaving. I started making plans, hoping you'd still want me to go with you." He popped the cork and filled the cups. "Here."

She took it and found a spot on one of the sleeping bags. "Giving up on your dream?"

"Rewriting it." Liam smiled and sat beside her. "Someone made an offer. It was more than I expected so I took it."

"Any regrets now that we're staying?"

He reached out, cupping her jaw, running his thumb over her cheek. "No. We'll find something else. A place that's ours, and build our dream home. A barn for your animals. Horses, goats, hogs, whatever you want."

"Sounds perfect," she said, turning her mouth and kissing the palm of his hand. "But we already have the land. I'm buying this place. I placed the offer as soon as I decided to sign the contract with Moore Timber."

"Honey, I'm not selling it to you."

"I have an accepted offer. That's as good as a contract.

And I trusted you to hold up your end of the bargain. You wouldn't go back on your word, would you?"

Liam laughed. "If you want it that badly, it's yours."

"Ours," she corrected. "And you know how I want to spend the first night at our dream-home site?"

He took her plastic cup and set it aside before drawing her into his arms and down onto the sleeping bag. "I have an idea."

She rolled on top of him, straddling his hips. Running her hands up his arms, she interlaced her fingers with his.

Liam smiled up at her. "Are you giving the orders?"

"No orders. Not this time." She leaned down, brushing her lips over his. "Just love me, Liam."

"Always, honey. Always."

Coming January 2015

HERO BY NIGHT
BOOK THREE: INDEPENDENCE FALLS

He was nobody's hero, until he landed in the wrong bed . . .

Armed with a golden retriever and a concealed weapons permit, Lena Clark is fighting for normal. She served her country, but the experience left her emotionally numb, afraid to be touched, and estranged from her career-military family. Staying in Independence Falls, and finding a job, seems like the first step to reclaiming her life until the town playboy stumbles into her bed . . .

Chad Summers is living his dream—helicopter logging by day and slipping between the sheets with Mrs. Right Now by night. Until his wild nights threaten his day job, leaving Chad with a choice: prove he can settle down or kiss his dream job goodbye. But after a party, Chad ends up in bed with the one woman in Independence Falls he can't have.

The playboy's touch ignited something in her. And Lena is determined to find out if it is the man, and his wicked demands in the bedroom, or if she's finally starting to heal. Chad is ready and willing to give into the primal desire to make Lena his at night—on one condition. By day, they pretend their relationship is real so he can show Independence Falls—and his boss—that he has shed his wild image. But their connection extends beyond the bedroom, threatening to turn their sham into reality—if Chad can prove he's the hero Lena needs night and day . . . forever.

About the Author

After several years on the other side of the publishing industry, SARA JANE STONE bid good-bye to her sales career to pursue her dream—writing romance novels. Sara Jane currently resides in Brooklyn, New York, with her very supportive real-life hero, two lively young children, and a lazy Burmese cat. Visit her online at www.sarajanestone. com, or find her on Facebook at www.facebook.com/ SaraJaneStone.

Join Sara Jane's newsletter to receive new release information, news about contests, giveaways, and more! To subscribe, visit www.sarajanestone.com and look for her newsletter sign-up form.

Visit www.AuthorTracker.com for exclusive information on your favorite HarperCollins authors.

Give in to your impulses . . .
Read on for a sneak peek at eight brand-new
e-book original tales of romance
from Avon Books.
Available now wherever e-books are sold.

THE COWBOY AND THE ANGEL
By T. J. Kline

FINDING MISS McFARLAND
THE WALLFLOWER WEDDING SERIES
By Vivienne Lorret

TAKE THE KEY AND LOCK HER UP
By Lena Diaz

DYLAN'S REDEMPTION
BOOK THREE: THE McBRIDES
By Jennifer Ryan

SINFUL REWARDS 1
A Billionaires and Bikers Novella
By Cynthia Sax

WHATEVER IT TAKES
A Trust No One Novel
By Dixie Lee Brown

HARD TO HOLD ON TO
A Hard Ink Novella
By Laura Kaye

KISS ME, CAPTAIN
A French Kiss Novel
By Gwen Jones

An Excerpt from

THE COWBOY AND THE ANGEL
By T. J. Kline

From author T. J. Kline comes the stunning
follow-up to *Rodeo Queen*. Reporter
Angela McCallister needs the scoop of her career
in order to save her father from the bad decisions
that have depleted their savings. When the
opportunity to spend a week at the
Findley Brothers ranch arises, she sees a chance
to get a behind-the-scenes scoop on rodeo. That
certainly doesn't include kissing the devastatingly
handsome and charming cowboy Derek Chandler,
who insists on calling her "Angel."

"Angela, call on line three."

"Can't you just handle it, Joe? I don't have time for this B.S." It was probably just another stupid mom calling, hoping Angela would feature her daughter's viral video in some feel-good news story. When was she ever going to get her break and find some hard-hitting news?

"They asked for you."

Angela sighed. Maybe if she left them listening to that horrible elevator music long enough, they'd hang up. Joe edged closer to her desk.

"Just pick up the damn phone and see what they want."

"Fine." She glared at him as she punched the button. The look she gave him belied the sweet tone of her voice. "Angela McCallister, how can I help you?"

Joe leaned against her cubical wall, listening to her part of the conversation. She waved at him irritably. It wasn't always easy when your boss was your oldest friend, and ex-boyfriend. He quirked a brow at her.

Go away, she mouthed.

"Are you really looking for new stories?"

She assumed the male voice on the line was talking about the calls the station ran at the ends of several news programs asking for stories of interest. Most of them wound up in her mental "ignore" file, but once in a while she'd found one worth pursuing.

"We're always looking for events and stories of interest to our local viewers." She rolled her eyes, reciting the words Joe had taught her early on in her career as a reporter. She was tired of pretending any of this sucking up was getting her anywhere. Viewers only saw her as a pretty face.

"I have a lead that might interest you." She didn't answer, waiting for the caller to elaborate. "There's a rodeo coming to town, and they are full of animal cruelty and abuse."

This didn't sound like a feel-good piece. The caller had her attention now. "Do you have proof?"

The voice gave a bitter laugh, sounding vaguely familiar. "Have you ever seen a rodeo? Electric prods, cinches wrapped around genitals, sharp objects placed under saddles to get horses to buck . . . it's all there."

She listened as the caller detailed several incidents at nearby rodeos where animals had to be euthanized due to injuries. Angela arched a brow, taking notes as the man gave her several websites she could research that backed the accusations.

"Can I contact you for more information?" She heard him hemming. "You don't have to give me your name. Maybe just a phone number or an email address where I can reach you?" The caller gave her both. "Do you mind if I ask one more question—why me?"

"Because you seem like you care about animal rights. That story you did about the stray kittens and the way you found them a home, it really showed who you were inside."

Angela barely remembered the story other than that Joe had forced it on her when she'd asked for one about a local politician sleeping with his secretary, reminding her that viewers saw her as their small-town sweetheart. She'd found herself reporting about a litter of stray kittens, smiling at the animal shelter as families adopted their favorites, and Jennifer Michaels had broken the infidelity story and was now anchoring at a station in Los Angeles. She was tired of this innocent, girl-next-door act.

"I'll see what I can do," she promised, deciding how to best pitch this story to Joe and whether it would be worth it at all.

An Excerpt from

FINDING MISS McFARLAND
The Wallflower Wedding Series
by Vivienne Lorret

Delany McFarland is on the hunt for a husband—
preferably one who needs her embarrassingly large
dowry more than a dutiful wife. Griffin Croft
hasn't been able to get Miss McFarland out of his
mind, but now that she's determined to hand over
her fortune to a rake, Griffin knows he must step
in. Yet when his noble intentions flee in a moment
of unexpected passion, his true course becomes
clear: tame Delaney's wild heart and save her from
a fate worse than death . . . a life without love.

She *had* been purposely avoiding him.

Griffin clasped his hands behind his back and began to pace around her in a circle. "Do you have spies informing you on my whereabouts at all times, or only for social gatherings?"

Miss McFarland watched his movements for a moment, but then she pursed those pink lips and smoothed the front of her cream gown. "I do what I must to avoid being seen at the same function with you. Until recently, I imagined we shared this unspoken agreement."

"Rumormongers rarely remember innocent bystanders."

She scoffed. "How nice for you."

"Yes, and until recently, I was under the impression that I came and went of my own accord. That my decisions were mine alone. Instead, I learn that every choice I make falls under your scrutiny." He was more agitated than angered. Not to mention intrigued and unaccountably aroused by her admission. During a season packed full of social engagements, she must require daily reports of his activities. Which begged the question, how often did she think of him? "Shall I quiz you on how I take my tea? Or if my valet prefers to tie my cravat into a barrel knot or horse collar?"

"I do not know, nor do I care, how you take your tea, Mr.

Croft," she said, and he clenched his teeth to keep from asking her to say it once more. "However, since I am something of an expert on fashion, I'd say that the elegant fall of the mail coach knot you're wearing this evening suits the structure of your face. The sapphire pin could make one imagine that your eyes are blue—"

"But you know differently."

Her cheeks went pink before she drew in a breath and settled her hand over her middle. Before he could stop the thought, he wondered whether she was experiencing the *fluttering* his sister had mentioned.

"You are determined to be disagreeable. I have made my attempts at civility, but now I am quite through with you. If you'll excuse me . . ." She started forward to leave.

He blocked her path, unable to forget what he'd heard when he first arrived. "I cannot let you go without a dire warning for your own benefit."

"If this is in regard to what you overheard—when you were eavesdropping on a *private matter*—I won't hear it."

He doubted she would listen to him if he meant to warn her about a great hole in the earth directly in her path either, but his conscience demanded he speak the words nonetheless. "Montwood is a desperate man, and you have put yourself in his power."

Her eyes flashed. "*That* is where you are wrong. I am the one with the fortune, ergo the one with the power."

How little she knew of men. "And what of your reputation?"

Her laugh did nothing to amuse him. "What I have left of my reputation will remain unscathed. He is not interested in my person. He only needs my fortune. In addition, as a second son, he does not require an heir; therefore, our living apart should not cause a problem with his family. And should he need *companionship*, he is free to find it elsewhere, so long as he's discreet."

"You sell yourself so easily, believing your worth is nothing more than your father's account ledger," he growled, his temper getting the better of him. He'd never lost control of it before, but for some reason this tested his limits. If *he* could see she was more than a sum of wealth, then *she* should damn well put a higher value on herself. "If you were my sister, I'd lock you in a convent for the rest of your days."

Miss McFarland stepped forward and pressed the tip of her manicured finger in between the buttons of his waistcoat. "I am *not* your sister, Mr. Croft. And thank the heavens for that gift, too. I can barely stand to be in the same room with you. You make it impossible to breathe, let alone think. Neither my lungs nor my stomach recalls how to function. Not only that, but you cause this terrible crackling sensation beneath my skin, and it feels like I'm about to catch fire." Her lips parted, and her small bosom rose and fell with each breath. "I do believe I loathe you to the very core of your being, Mr. Croft."

Somewhere between the first *Mis-ter-Croft* and the last, he'd lost all sense.

Because in the very next moment, he gripped her shoulders, hauled her against him, and crushed his mouth to hers.

An Excerpt from

TAKE THE KEY AND LOCK HER UP

by Lena Diaz

As a trained assassin for EXIT Inc—a top-secret
mercenary group—Devlin "Devil" Buchanan isn't
afraid to take justice into his own hands. But with
EXIT Inc closing in and several women's lives on
the line, Detective Emily O'Malley and Devlin
must work together to find the missing women and
clear both their names before time runs out . . .
and their key to freedom is thrown away.

"I want to talk to you about what you do at EXIT."

"No."

She blinked. "No?" Her cell phone beeped. She grabbed it impatiently and took the call. A few seconds later she shoved the phone back in her pocket. "Tuck's outside. The SWAT team is set up and ready to cover us in case those two yokels decide to start shooting again. The area is secure. Let's go." She headed toward the door.

"Wait."

She turned, her brows raised in question.

He braced his legs in a wide stance and crossed his arms. "If I'm not under arrest, there's no reason for me to go to the police station."

Her mouth firmed into a tight line. "You're not under arrest only if you agree to the deal I offered. The man who killed Shannon Garrett and the unidentified victims in that basement is holding at least two other women right now, doing God only knows what to them. All I'm asking is that you answer some questions to help me find them, so I can save their lives. Doesn't that mean anything to you?"

Of course it did. But he also knew Kelly Parker, and anyone with her, couldn't be saved by Emily and her fellow cops. It was becoming increasingly clear that Kelly was the bait in a trap to catch *him*. The killer would keep her alive, maybe even provide proof of life at some point, to lure Devlin to wherever she was being held. Did he care about her suffering? Absolutely. Which meant he had to come up with a plan to save her without charging full steam ahead and getting himself killed. Because once the killer eliminated his main prey—Devlin—he'd have no reason to keep either of the women alive.

He braced himself for his next lie. If Emily thought he was bad to supposedly get a woman pregnant and abandon her, she was going to despise him after this next one.

"Finding and saving those women is your job," he said. "I have other things to do that are a lot more fun than sitting in an interrogation room."

The shocked, disgusted look that crossed her face was no worse than the way he felt inside. Like a jerk, and a damn coward. But if sacrificing his pride kept her safe, so be it. He had to get outside and offer himself as bait to lead his enemies away from the diner before she went out the front. He strode past her to the bathroom door.

"Stop, Devlin, or I'll shoot."

He slowly turned around. Seeing his sexy little detective pointing a gun at him again seemed every kind of wrong, especially when his blood was still raging from the hot kiss they'd just shared.

"Seriously?" he said, faking shock. "You're drawing on an unarmed man? *Again?* What will Drier say about that? Or Alex? I smell a lawsuit."

She stomped her foot in frustration.

The urge to laugh at her childish action had him clenching his teeth. She was the perfect blend of innocence, naiveté, and just plain stubbornness. Before he did something they'd both regret—like kissing her again—he slipped out of the bathroom.

A quick side trip through the kitchen too quickly for anyone to even question his presence, and he was down the back hallway, standing at the rear exit. Now all he had to do was make it to some kind of cover—without getting shot—and lead Cougar and his handler away from Emily, all without a weapon of his own to return fire.

Simple. No problem. He shook his head and cursed his decision to go to the police station this morning. Then again, if he hadn't, he wouldn't have gotten to kiss Emily. If he were killed in the next few minutes, at least he'd die with that intoxicating memory still lingering on his lips.

He cracked the door open and scanned the nearby buildings. Then he flung the door wide and took off running.

An Excerpt from

DYLAN'S REDEMPTION
Book Three: The McBrides
by Jennifer Ryan

From *New York Times* bestselling author Jennifer
Ryan, the McBrides of Fallbrook return with
Dylan McBride, the new sheriff. Jessie Thompson
had one hell of a week. Dylan McBride, the boy
she loved, skipped town without a word. Then her
drunk of a father tried to kill her, and she fled
Fallbrook, vowing never to return. Eight years
later, her father is dead, and Jessie reluctantly
goes home—only to come face-to-face with
the man who shattered her heart. A man who,
for nearly a decade, believed she was dead.

Standing over her sleeping brother, she held the pitcher in one hand and the cup of coffee in the other. She poured the cold water over her brother's face and chest. He sat bolt upright and yelled, "What the hell!"

Brian held a hand to his dripping head and one to his stomach. He probably had a splitting headache to go with his rotten gut. As far as Jessie was concerned, he deserved both.

"Good morning, brother. Nice of you to rise and shine."

Brian wiped a hand over his wet face and turned to sit on the sodden couch. His blurry eyes found Jessie standing over him. His mouth dropped open, and his eyes went round before he gained his voice.

"You're dead. I've hit that bottom people talk about. I'm dreaming, hallucinating after a night of drinking. It can't be you. You're gone and it's all my fault." He covered his face with his hands. Tears filled his voice, his pain and sorrow sharp and piercing. She refused to let it get to her, despite her guilt for making him believe she'd died. Brian needed a good ass-kicking, not a sympathetic ear.

"You're going to wish I died when I get through with you, you miserable drunk. What the hell happened to you?" She handed over the mug of coffee and shoved it up to his mouth to make him take a sip. Reality setting in, he needed the coffee and a shower before he'd concentrate and focus on her and what she had in store for him.

"Don't yell, my head is killing me." He pressed the heel of his hand to his eye, probably hoping his brain wouldn't explode.

Jessie sat on the coffee table in front of her brother, between his knees, and leaned forward with her elbows braced on her thighs.

"Listen to me, brother dear. It's past time you cleaned up your act. Starting today, you are going to quit drinking yourself into a stupor. You're going to take care of your wife and child. You're going to show up for work on Monday morning clear eyed and ready to earn an honest day's pay."

"Work? I don't have any job lined up for Monday."

"Yes, you do. I gave Marilee the information. You report to James on Monday at the new housing development going up on the outskirts of town. You'll earn a decent paycheck and have medical benefits for your family.

"The old man left you the house. I'll go over tomorrow after the funeral to see what needs to be done to make it livable for you and Marilee. I, big brother, am going to make you be the man you used to be, because I can't stand to see you turn into the next Buddy Thompson. You got that?" She'd yelled it at him to get his attention and to reinforce the fact that he'd created his condition. His eyes rolled back in his head, and he groaned in pain, all the reward she needed.

"If you don't show up for work on Monday, I'm coming after you. And I'll keep coming until you get it through that thick head of yours: you are not him. You're better than that. So get your ass up, take a shower, mow the lawn, kiss your wife, tell her you love her and you aren't going to be this asshole you've turned into anymore. You hear me?"

"Your voice is ringing in my head." He stared into his coffee cup, but glanced up to say, "You look good. Life's apparently turned out all right for you."

Jessie shrugged that off, focused more on the lost look in Brian's round, sad eyes.

"I thought you died that night. I left and he killed you. Where have you been?"

"Around. Mostly Solomon. I have a house about twenty miles outside of Fallbrook."

"You do?" The surprise lit his face.

"I started my life over. It's time you did the same."

An Excerpt from

SINFUL REWARDS 1
A Billionaires and Bikers Novella
by Cynthia Sax

Belinda "Bee" Carter is a good girl; at least, that's
what she tells herself. And a good girl deserves
a nice guy—just like the gorgeous and moody
billionaire Nicolas Rainer. Or so she thinks,
until she takes a look through her telescope
and sees a naked, tattooed man on the balcony
across the courtyard. He has been watching
her, and that makes him all the more enticing.
But when a mysterious and anonymous text
message dares her to do something bad, she
must decide if she is really the good girl she has
always claimed to be, or if she's willing to risk
everything for her secret fantasy of being watched.

An Avon Red Novella

I'd told Cyndi I'd never use it, that it was an instrument purchased by perverts to spy on their neighbors. She'd laughed and called me a prude, not knowing that I was one of those perverts, that I secretly yearned to watch and be watched, to care and be cared for.

If I'm cautious, and I'm always cautious, she'll never realize I used her telescope this morning. I swing the tube toward the bench and adjust the knob, bringing the mysterious object into focus.

It's a phone. Nicolas's phone. I bounce on the balls of my feet. This is a sign, another declaration from fate that we belong together. I'll return Nicolas's much-needed device to him. As a thank you, he'll invite me to dinner. We'll talk. He'll realize how perfect I am for him, fall in love with me, marry me.

Cyndi will find a fiancé also—everyone loves her—and we'll have a double wedding, as sisters of the heart often do. It'll be the first wedding my family has had in generations.

Everyone will watch us as we walk down the aisle. I'll wear a strapless white Vera Wang mermaid gown with organza and lace details, crystal and pearl embroidery accents, the bodice fitted, and the skirt hemmed for my shorter height. My hair will be swept up. My shoes—

Voices murmur outside the condo's door, the sound piercing my delightful daydream. I swing the telescope upward, not wanting to be caught using it. The snippets of conversation drift away.

I don't relax. If the telescope isn't positioned in the same way as it was last night, Cyndi will realize I've been using it. She'll tease me about being a fellow pervert, sharing the story, embellished for dramatic effect, with her stern, serious dad—or, worse, with Angel, that snobby friend of hers.

I'll die. It'll be worse than being the butt of jokes in high school because that ridicule was about my clothes and this will center on the part of my soul I've always kept hidden. It'll also be the truth, and I won't be able to deny it. I am a pervert.

I have to return the telescope to its original position. This is the only acceptable solution. I tap the metal tube.

Last night, my man-crazy roommate was giggling over the new guy in three-eleven north. The previous occupant was a gray-haired, bowtie-wearing tax auditor, his luxurious accommodations supplied by Nicolas. The most exciting thing he ever did was drink his tea on the balcony.

According to Cyndi, the new occupant is a delicious piece of man candy—tattooed, buff, and head-to-toe lickable. He was completing armcurls outside, and she enthusiastically counted his reps, oohing and aahing over his bulging biceps, calling to me to take a look.

I resisted that temptation, focusing on making macaroni and cheese for the two of us, the recipe snagged from the diner my mom works in. After we scarfed down dinner, Cyndi licking her plate clean, she left for the club and hasn't returned.

Three-eleven north is the mirror condo to ours. I

straighten the telescope. That position looks about right, but then, the imitation UGGs I bought in my second year of college looked about right also. The first time I wore the boots in the rain, the sheepskin fell apart, leaving me barefoot in Economics 201.

Unwilling to risk Cyndi's friendship on "about right," I gaze through the eyepiece. The view consists of rippling golden planes, almost like . . .

Tanned skin pulled over defined abs.

I blink. It can't be. I take another look. A perfect pearl of perspiration clings to a puckered scar. The drop elongates more and more, stretching, snapping. It trickles downward, navigating the swells and valleys of a man's honed torso.

No. I straighten. This is wrong. I shouldn't watch our sexy neighbor as he stands on his balcony. If anyone catches me . . .

Parts 1 and 2 available now!

An Excerpt from

WHATEVER IT TAKES
A Trust No One Novel
by Dixie Lee Brown

Assassin Alex Morgan will do anything to save
an innocent life—especially if it means rescuing
a child from a hell like the one she endured. But
going undercover as husband and wife, with
none other than the disarmingly sexy Detective
Nate Sanders, may be a little more togetherness
than she can handle. Nate's willing to face
anything if it means protecting Alex. She may
have been on her own once, but Nate has one
more mission: to stay by her side—forever.

What was Alex doing in that bar? She had to be following him. It was too much of a coincidence any other way. Nate nearly flinched when he replayed the image of her dropping Daniels and then turning on those goons getting ready to shoot up the bar. Shit! Was she suicidal along with everything else? Anger, tinged with dread, did a slow burn under his collar. He needed to know what motivated Alex Morgan . . . and he needed to know now.

He clenched his teeth, whipped his bike into an alley, and cut the engine. If she was bent on getting herself killed, there was no fucking way it was happening on his turf.

She dismounted, uncertainty in her expression. As soon as she stepped out of the way, he swung his leg over and got in her face. "Take it off." He pointed to the helmet.

Not waiting for her to remove it all the way, he started in. "What in the name of all that's holy were you thinking back there? You could have gotten yourself killed."

A sad smile swept her face and something in her eyes—a momentary hardening—gave him a clue to the answer he was fairly certain she'd never speak aloud. Ty had told him the highlights of her story. Joe had freed Alex from a life of slavery in a dark, dismal hole in Hong Kong. From the haunted look in her eyes, however, Nate would bet she hadn't completely dealt with the aftermath. His first impression had been more right than he wanted to admit. It was quite likely that she nursed a dangerous little death wish, and that's what had prompted her actions at the bar.

His anger receded, and a wave of protectiveness rolled over him, but he was powerless to take away the pain staring back at him. He could make a stab at shielding her from the world, but how could he stop the hell that raged inside this woman? Why did she matter so much to him? Hell, logic flew out the window a long time ago. He didn't know why—only that she *did*. With frustration driving him, he stepped closer, pushing her against the bike. Her moist lips drew his gaze, and an overwhelming desire to kiss her set fire to his blood.

She stiffened and wariness flooded her eyes.

He should have stopped there, but another step put him in contact with her, and he was burning with need. He pulled her closer and gently slid his fingers through her hair, then stroked his thumb across her bottom lip.

Her breath escaped in uneven gasps and a tiny bit of tongue appeared, sliding quickly over the lip he'd just touched. Fear, trepidation, longing paraded across her face. Ty's warning sounded in his ears again—she was dangerous, maybe even disturbed—but even if that was true, Nate wasn't sure it made any difference to him.

"Don't be afraid." *Shit!* Immediately, he regretted his words. This woman wasn't afraid of anything. Distrustful . . . yes. Afraid? He didn't even want to know what could scare her.

Her eyes softened and warmed, and she stepped into him, pressing her firm body against his. He caught her around the waist and aligned his hips to hers. Ignoring the words of caution in his head, he bent ever so slowly and covered her mouth with his. Softly caressing her lips and tasting her sweetness, he forgot for a moment that they stood in an alley in a questionable area of Portland, that he barely knew this woman, and that they'd just left the scene of a real-life nightmare.

He'd longed to kiss her since the first time they'd met. She'd insulted his car that day, and not even that had been enough to get his mind off her lips. Good timing or bad—kissing her and holding her in his arms was long overdue.

An Excerpt from

HARD TO HOLD ON TO
A Hard Ink Novella
by *Laura Kaye*

From *New York Times* and *USA Today* bestselling author Laura Kaye comes a hot, sexy novella to tie in with her Hard Ink series. When "Easy" meets Jenna, he has finally found someone to care for, and he will do anything to keep her safe.

As the black F150 truck shot through the night-darkened streets of one of Baltimore's grittiest neighborhoods, Edward Cantrell cradled the unconscious woman in his arms like she was the only thing tethering him to life. And right at this moment, she was.

Jenna Dean was bloodied and bruised after having been kidnapped by the worst sort of trash the day before, but she was still an incredibly beautiful woman. And saving her from the clutches of a known drug dealer and human trafficker was without question the most important thing he'd done in more than a year.

He should have felt happy—or at least happier—but those feelings were foreign countries for Easy. Had been for a long time.

Easy, for his initials: E.C. The nickname had been the brainchild years before of Shane McCallan, one of his Army Special Forces teammates, who now sat at the other end of the big back seat, wrapped so far around Jenna's older sister, Sara, that they might need the Jaws of Life to pull them apart. Not that Easy blamed them. When you walked through fire and somehow came out the other side in one piece, you gave thanks and held tight to the things that mattered.

Because too often, when shit got critical, the ones you loved didn't make it out the other side. And then you wished you'd given more thanks and held on harder before the fires ever started raging around you in the first place.

Easy would fucking know.

The pickup paused as a gate *whirr*ed out of the way, then the tires crunched over gravel and came to a rough stop. Easy lifted his gaze from Jenna's fire-red hair and too-pale face to find that they were home—or, at least, where he was calling home right now. Out his window, the redbrick industrial building housing Hard Ink Tattoo loomed in the darkness, punctuated here and there by the headlights of some of the Raven Riders bikers who'd helped Easy and his teammates rescue Jenna and take down the gangbangers who'd grabbed her.

Talk about strange bedfellows.

Five former Green Berets and twenty-odd members of an outlaw motorcycle club. Then again, maybe not so strange. Easy and his buddies had been drummed out of the Army under suspicious, other-than-honorable circumstances. Disgraced, dishonored, disowned. Didn't matter that his team had been seriously set up for a big fall. In the eyes of the US government and the world, the five of them weren't any better than the bikers they'd allied themselves with so that they'd have a fighting chance against the much bigger and better-armed Church gang. And, when you cut right down to it, maybe his guys weren't any better. After all, they'd gone total vigilante in their effort to clear their names, identify and take down their enemies, and clean up the collateral damage that occurred along the way.

Like Jenna.

"Easy? *Easy?* Hey, *E?*"

An Excerpt from

KISS ME, CAPTAIN
A French Kiss Novel
by Gwen Jones

In the fun and sexy follow-up to *Wanted: Wife,*
French billionaire and CEO of Mercier Shipping
Marcel Mercier puts his playboy lifestyle
on hold to handle a PR nightmare in the
US, but sparks fly when he meets the
passionate captain of his newest ship . . .

"**O**f course I realize he's your brother-in-law," Dani said, grinning most maliciously as she dragged the chains across the deck to the mainmast. "In fact I'm counting on it as my express delivery system." She wrapped a double length of chain around her waist. "My apologies for shamelessly exploiting you."

"Seriously?" Julie laughed. "Trust me, I'll try not to feel compromised."

"Like me," Dani said, her hair as red as the bloody blister of a sun rising over the Delaware. She yanked another length of chain around the mast. "But what can *I* do. I'm just a *woman*."

"And I'm just a media whore," Julie said. "And a bastard is a bastard is a bastard." She nodded to her cameraman, flexing her shoulders as she leveled her gaze into the lens. "How far would you go to save *your* job?"

Two days later
L'hôtel Croisette Beach
Cannes

*P*ineapple, Marcel Mercier deduced, drifting awake under the noonday sun. A woman's scent was always the first thing he noticed, as in the subtle fragrance of her soap, her perfumed pulse points, the lingering vestiges of her shampoo.

Mon Dieu. How he loved women.

"Marcel," he heard, feeling a silky leg slide against his own.

He opened his eyes to his *objet d'affection* for the past three days. *"Bébé . . ."* he growled, brushing his lips across hers as she curled into him.

"Marcel, *mon amour*," she cooed, fairly beaming with joy. *"Tu m'as fait tellement heureuse."*

"What?" he said, nuzzling her neck. Her pineapple scent was driving him insane.

She slid her hand between his legs. "I *said* you've made me very happy." Then she smiled. No—beamed.

He froze, mid-nibble. Oh no. Oh *no*.

She kissed him, her eyes bright. "I don't care what Paris says—I'm wearing my *grand-mère's* Brussels lace to our wedding. You wouldn't mind, would you?"

He stared at her. Had he really gone and done what he swore he'd never do again? He really needed to lay off the absinthe cocktails. "Mirabel, I didn't mean to—"

"Why did you leave me last night?" she said, falling back against the chaise, her bare breasts heaving above the tiny triangle of her string bikini bottom. "You left so fast the maids are still scrubbing scorch marks from the carpet."

Merde. He really ought to get his *dard* registered as a lethal weapon. He affected an immediate blitheness. "I had to take a call," he said—his standard alibi—raking his gaze over her. She really was quite the babe. "I didn't want to wake you."

All at once she went to full-blown *en garde*, shoving her face into his. "*Really*. More like you couldn't wait to get away from me. And after last night? After what you asked me?" Her enormous breasts rose, fell, her gaze slicing into his. "You said . . . You. *Loved*. Me."

Had he? *Christ*. He needed to diffuse this. So he switched gears, summoning all his powers of seduction. "Mirabel. *Chère*." He smiled—lethally, he knew—cradling her chin as he nipped the corner of her mouth. "But that call turned into another, then three, and before you knew it . . ." He traced his finger over the bloom of her breasts and down into the sweet, sweet cavern between them, his tongue edging her lip until she shivered like an ingénue. "You know damn well there's only one way to wake a gorgeous girl like you."

"You should've come back," she said softly, a bit disarmed, though the edge still lingered in her voice. "You just should have." She barely breathed it.

"How, *bébé*?" He licked the hollow behind her ear, and when she jolted, Marcel nearly snickered in triumph. Watching women falling *for* him nearly outranked falling *into* them. "Should I have slipped under the door?" he said, feathering kisses across her jawline. "Or maybe climbed up the balcony, calling 'Juliet? Juliet?' "

She arched her neck and sighed, a deep blush staining her overripe breasts. Marcel fought a rush of disappointment.

Truly, they were all so predictable. A bit of adulatory strok-
ing and it was like they performed on cue. She pressed against
his chest as he tugged the bikini string at her hip, her mouth
opening in a tiny gasp.

"Mar-cel . . ." she purred.

He sighed inwardly. It was almost too easy. And that was
the scary part.